01

The stage was dark. Just to the left of the stage, a tall, slender figure stood with a Bible in his hand. He took a deep breath in and walked out. The shiny floor reflected slivers of light while the audience sat in silence. Seconds after the man stepped onto the platform, bright, beaming light filled the stage. A tall round table was set up next to the man, and on it, he placed his Bible.

In the front row of the audience, a boy sat watching the man's every move, captivated by him. The fifteen-year-old, Austin, loved going to church. He sat in the front row every single Sunday at nine A.M. and watched Pastor John Anderson preach.

Austin had wanted to be a preacher since he was 5 years old. Most kids dreamt of being doctors and teachers, but Austin wasn't like most kids. Sure, he had friends and hobbies, but he also had a Bible that had been read so many times the ink was fading and the binding was falling apart. Austin radiated kindness and humility to everyone he crossed paths with.

Pastor Anderson started to speak on the parable of the lost sheep. As always he highlighted parts of the story that had never crossed anyone's mind. John Anderson was a bright and intelligent man. He had the look of a college professor in his late forties. His light brown hair had streaks of gray in it and his beard emulated a similar look. He was professional and yet he had a tender heart.

He would always leave the congregation of Westeast church saying, "That was one of the best sermons I've ever heard." This Sunday was no different. After the closing worship song, Austin and his family walked out into the atrium where about 5,000 of the 15,000 weekly attendees stood talking to each other.

"Hey, Mom, I'm gonna go wait in the car." Austin gripped his black leather Bible in one hand and ran his other hand through his wavy blondish brown hair.

"Are you sure? Me and dad won't be too long." Austin's mom, Kim, looked at her son with a sad smile.

"Yeah, I'm sure." Austin turned away and headed for the car.

He opened the door to the passenger side and sat down, propping his legs up on the dashboard. He fingered a white envelope that was sticking out of his Bible. It had Pastor Anderson written on the front in a sloppy scrawl. Inside was a letter that Austin had written the night before, and at home, there was a shoebox full of letters he had written every other Saturday night for the past two years.

After ten minutes of sitting in the car alone, Kim and Ben walked out to their blue *Toyota* minivan.

"Bud, backseat now." Ben looked at his son with a playful smile as he held open the passenger side door and motioned for Austin to get out.

Austin let out a slight groan and moved to the backseat. Kim slid into the driver's seat and adjusted the rearview mirror before starting the car and driving home. Once they pulled into the garage Austin was practically unbuckled and opening the door.

He ran up to his room and retrieved the shoebox full of letters from under his bed. He took this week's letter, placed it on top of the stack, and then proceeded to shut the box and shove it back under his bed. Except for a few dirty socks lying on the floor, his room was cleaner than most teenage boys. An old family portrait hung over Austin's bed. Across the room, an old-fashioned wooden desk stood littered with half-read books and half-written papers.

Austin positioned himself in the middle of his queen size bed and opened his Bible to the parable of the lost sheep. Sometimes Austin would lie in bed and stare up at the ceiling and think about how he felt like the lost sheep. Alone and scared but still loved and cared for. This summer was a lonely one, all of his friends had taken exotic vacations with their families, but Austin's parents had decided to stay home this year.

A soft knock on the door interrupted his thoughts.

"Come in." Austin sat up in his bed and set his Bible aside.

"We're about to eat dinner, wanna think about joining us?" Kim stepped into the room and picked up a piece of trash next to her foot.

"Yeah, what are we having?" Austin stood up and started to follow his mom downstairs.

"Lasagna and Caesar salad, your favorite!"

Austin smiled, he loved Caesar salad. The table was set for a quiet dinner. There was a small candle in the center of the table and plates of food at everyone's spot. In a family of three, everybody sat next to each other so each meal had an intimate feeling that families of four or five would never experience.

After eating a few forkfuls of warm, cheesy lasagna, Ben started talking about the family's plans for the week, "I was thinking that after I get back from work on Wednesday we could meet some friends for dinner or something. Just to get out of the house."

"Austin has a doctor's appointment on Wednesday afternoon, so it would have to be a later dinner." Kim pushed a piece of her silky brown hair behind her ear. Her hazel eyes shimmered from the candlelight.

"A doctor's appointment?" Ben scratched his recently shaven face and looked up from his food.

"Yes, just a check-up and sports physical."

Austin moved his fork around his plate in a slow circular motion and let out a slight yawn, "I'm kinda tired, I think I'll head to bed soon… If that's alright."

Kim glanced at her silver watch, "It is getting late, that's fine. We'll come to say goodnight in a little while."

Austin went up to his room and found a pair of basketball shorts and an oversized t-shirt to wear to bed. He brushed his teeth in the tiny bathroom that was connected to his bedroom, and after quickly rinsing his face he glanced in the mirror. Staring back at him was a tall and slender boy with green eyes that could light up a whole room.

“God, hey… It’s been a long day. Can we talk?” Austin hopped into his bed and continued to talk quietly to his heavenly father.

Kim pushed open the door to Austin’s room and Ben came in behind her.

“Goodnight sweetheart. I love you.” Kim planted a soft kiss on Austin’s forehead.

“Love you too mom.”

“Goodnight bud.” Ben patted Austin’s knee and followed Kim out of the room, leaving their son to continue his prayers before he closed his eyes and drifted off to sleep.

⤖ ⤖ ⤖

“Austin, are you ready to go?” Kim called to Austin from the door frame that connected the house to the garage.

"COOOMING!!" Austin shouted back from inside his room.

He shoved on a pair of already tied *Nike* tennis shoes and bounded down the stairs to the garage.

His mom was already waiting for him in the car. He slid into the front seat and kicked his legs up in front of him.

"Feet down." Kim pointed to his feet as she started to back out.

"Ughhh, yes ma'am." Austin reluctantly put his feet down and folded his arms across his chest. Without hitting a single red light, Austin and Kim made it to the doctor's office in record time.

Because Austin was still a minor, he saw a pediatrician, and like most pediatrician's offices, it was decorated like something out of an old cartoon. There was blue wallpaper with little hot air balloons all over it and plastic red chairs that filled the waiting area.

A few minutes passed before a nurse came out and called for "Austin O'Conor."

Austin and his mom got up and followed the nurse to a small room that was decorated to match the waiting area, only this room had a long table for the patient to lay on.

"Doctor Blunt will be right with you." The nurse smiled and closed the door to the little room.

"I hate going to the doctor." Austin kicked his feet back and forth as they waited for the doctor.

"Most people do, but remember that one sermon Pastor Anderson preached about the African woman who didn't have a doctor and her baby didn't make it because there was no one to help?" Kim looked into Austin's eyes, anytime she brought up Pastor Anderson, she was sure to get his attention.

"Of course I remember it, I remember all of his sermons. I guess you're right. Sorry for complaining." Austin's tone was sincere, as was his apology.

A quick knock on the door signaled that Doctor Blunt was ready.

"Hey Austin!" Doctor Blunt was in her early twenties and fresh out of medical school at the top of her class. Not only was she skilled medically, she was also extremely personable.

"Hi." Austin stopped kicking his legs and made eye contact with Doctor Blunt.

"So, are you playing any sports this year?" Doctor Blunt sat down on a round stool with wheels on it.

"Just running track and cross country." Austin wasn't the fastest or most skilled runner on the team, but he never gave up and that's what made him a valuable player.

"Very good. If you could sit up and scoot towards the edge of the table, I'll take a quick listen to your heart and lungs." She breathed warm air onto her stethoscope and put it up to Austin's chest.

After a few minutes of listening, Doctor Blunt turned to Kim and frowned.

"I don't like to make conclusions without evidence, so I won't, but I hear something in Austin's lungs that concerns me. It's hard to say what it is now, however, I’m going to recommend you get a chest x-ray.”

Before Doctor Blunt had time to say anything else, Kim let out a small gasp.

“It could be nothing, although that seems unlikely based on what I heard. I’ll order an x-ray and I suggest you get it taken care of as soon as possible. If nothing’s wrong then you can be at ease and if there is something you’ll be able to treat it as soon as possible.”

“Is… is it bad?” Kim tapped her foot nervously against the filthy tile floor.

“As I said, it's hard to know without an x-ray. I wouldn’t worry about it too much.”

Kim slowly nodded her head. Doctor Blunt finished the examination, but it was all a blur for Austin and his mom. After a moment of silence in the car Austin spoke up, “Umm… are we still gonna meet dad for dinner?”

Kim let out a breathy sigh, “Yeah, we…uh… we can't get the x-ray until tomorrow morning.”

"Okay." Austin looked at his reflection in the side rearview mirror, there were tears in his eyes.

Kim pulled into the restaurant, where she and Austin somberly walked in to meet Ben. He greeted them with a big smile. A couple that Ben and Kim were friends with were sitting with Ben.

"Austin, I haven't told your dad the news yet," Kim whispered to him as they approached the table.

Austin nodded to his mom and sat down next to his dad.

"Hey bud! How was the doctor's appointment." Ben took a sip of his water through a small black straw.

"Fine I guess." Austin shrugged and placed his napkin in his lap.

"You remember Shawna and Josh, right?" Ben directed his question to Austin.

"Yep, nice to see you guys again."

Shawna was sitting across from Austin and Josh was sitting at the end of the table. The waiter quickly took the table's orders and left them to talk. The conversation was focused on an upcoming election for governor and other various heads of state. When the food came out, Austin devoured his spaghetti and meatballs within minutes.

"Well, it was really nice to talk to you two," Ben stood up and shook hands with Josh.

"Yeah, it was good to see you all. We'll have to do this again sometime soon," Josh grabbed his box of leftovers from the table.

Kim hugged Shawna and waved goodbye to Josh as they all walked to their cars. Almost immediately after leaving the restaurant, Ben asked Austin what was wrong. Austin silently marveled at how his dad knew something was up, but before he had a chance to respond, Kim explained what Doctor Blunt had told them earlier.

"Is he going to be okay?" Panic rose in Ben's voice.

"I have no idea. It's just so unexpected. Austin's never had health problems before. I don't think it's genetic. How does this kind of thing even happen?" Kim bore the face of a worried mother as she spoke.

"It's like something out of a movie." Ben tried to focus on the road, but his mind was running through all the possible scenarios that could come of this situation.

Austin quietly sat in the backseat while his parents continued to talk about him like he wasn't even there. Questions about the future consumed his thoughts throughout the drive home. His room was a welcome comfort after the day's events.

He settled into his bed and flipped through his Bible until he got to Phillipians four verse six. At some point in time, he had highlighted the verse neon yellow, and now the words stared up at him: "Do not be anxious about anything, but in every situation, by prayer and petition, with thanksgiving, present your requests to God."

How could he not be anxious when his future was unknown? But God had seen him through tough times before, this wouldn't be any different, would it?

Doubts and fears flooded Austin's mind, and yet the verse from Philippians brought him a peace that surpassed all of the things troubling him. Austin began to pray and ask God for clarity and strength. Half an hour later, he drifted off to sleep.

Come morning, Austin couldn't bring himself to eat breakfast. The pending x-ray had put everyone on edge. Kim took a quick shower before accompanying Austin to the radiology clinic. The receptionist behind the front desk checked Austin in and handed Kim a clipboard full of paperwork to fill out.

"Are you currently experiencing any symptoms of diabetes?" Kim looked at Austin before checking the "no" box on the paper.

"No. Why do they even ask questions like that?" Austin rolled his eyes and went back to scrolling through his *Instagram* feed.

A nurse walked into the waiting room and called Austin back. Kim wasn't allowed to go with Austin, so she squeezed his hand and told him to be brave.

Once inside the x-ray imaging room, Austin had to put on a light blue hospital gown. The radiologist instructed him to stand in front of the x-ray machine that would take the pictures. He told Austin to stay still and after a few loud clicks and beeps, it was over.

"You can go sit in that room over there and we'll tell your mom to come back," A nurse with a heavy southern drawl directed Austin to a stereotypical-looking consultation room.

Austin situated himself in a black cushioned chair while he waited for his mom.

"How'd it go?" Kim walked into the room and sat down next to Austin.

"Good, I think. The nurse said to wait in here and then I think they'll tell us the results." To help calm his nerves, Austin took some deep breaths and gently ran his fingers through his hair.

"Excuse me, are you Austin?" A tall man poked his head into the room where Kim and Austin were sitting.

Austin nodded and the man came in and sat down at a desk across from Kim.

“I’m the head radiologist here, my name is Cooper Sloss. I took a look at your pictures and I see a few things that concern me. I’ll send these to your primary doctor, and they’ll refer you to a pulmonologist.” Cooper clacked away on the keyboard as he input information.

“Can you give us an idea of what could be wrong?” Kim grabbed a piece of paper and a pen from her purse to write down whatever information Cooper gave her.

“Sure,”Cooper turned away from the computer so he was facing Kim, “From what I can tell it looks like it could be pulmonary alveolar proteinosis or maybe severe asthma. I’m leaning towards pulmonary alveolar proteinosis, and I think your pulmonologist would agree with me.”

“What is that?” Kim looked up from her piece of paper.

“I don’t know much about it, but it’s a rare disease that can be life-threatening. If I remember correctly, the most common symptom is breathlessness." Cooper folded his hands in front of him, "I would recommend seeing a pulmonologist as soon as possible. In the meantime, I'll send these over to your pediatrician."

"Thanks for all your help." Kim smiled at Cooper as she and Austin got up and started walking back to the entrance.

Once Austin and Kim got home, they went to the living room where Kim started to research what the radiologist had told her. Austin situated himself on the couch and flipped through the *Netflix* homepage until he found something that looked interesting.

The sound of the garage opening signaled that Ben was back from work. Austin quickly turned off the TV. Ben knew something was wrong the second he walked through the door. Kim's eyes looked red and puffy, and Austin rarely watched TV by himself.

"What did I miss?" Ben set down his work bag on the hardwood floor.

"Come sit down." Kim patted the couch cushion next to her.

Ben sat down, but he didn't sit back like he normally would. Instead, he leaned forward and rested his elbows on his knees.

"The x-rays showed that Austin has a rare disease called Pulmonary Alveolar Proteinosis also known as PAP." Tears formed in Kim's eyes, making it hard for her to talk without crying.

"How serious is it?" Ben put his arm around Kim.

"I don't know…" Kim bit her lip in an effort to try to keep from crying, but it didn't work, "Please excuse me." Kim swiftly walked to the bathroom and shut the door behind her.

"Austin…I…I'll be in the kitchen if you need me." Ben silently ambled out of the living room.

Austin went up to his bedroom and after praying for a while he shut his eyes and fell asleep. At some point, his mom opened the door to find him sleeping peacefully.

She went back downstairs to the primary suite where Ben was sitting in bed.

"Was Austin awake?" Ben lowered his reading glasses and looked up at Kim.

"No, he was sound asleep."

"I'm worried about him. I've never seen him this down." Ben waited for a response from Kim, but all he heard was her softly crying. "It's okay, I've got you." Ben wrapped his arms around Kim.

When Kim's tears slowed, Ben turned the light off and said goodnight to Kim. She returned the sentiment and added that she loved him.

Friday afternoon held a visit to the pulmonologist. Ben had work, so Kim took Austin to the appointment. For the third day in a row, the two sat in a dull waiting room with little to do. Thankfully the doctor was able to see Austin within twenty minutes of waiting.

He shook hands with Austin and Kim and then introduced himself. His name was Steve or Doctor Davis to his patients. The first thing Austin noted about him was his gray beard and his piercing blue eyes. Although some might perceive him to be intimidating, Austin took an immediate liking to him.

"I just want to start by saying that I am so sorry this happened to you all. I see patients all the time who are faced with sudden, unexpected diagnoses." Steve pulled his stethoscope off of his neck to listen to Austin's breathing.

Austin breathed in and out whenever Steve told him to. It was only a minute before Steve put his stethoscope away.

"I don't know what you've been told up to this point, but after reviewing the x-rays and listening to Austin breathe, I can say without a doubt it's Pulmonary Alveolar Proteinosis or PAP."

Kim barely let him finish speaking before she interrupted with a question, "Please tell us more Doctor Davis, we don't know much about it, and to be quite honest we're not sure what to do."

"PAP is basically a disease where your body doesn't make all the blood cells it needs to. The symptoms will begin with very unnoticeable shortness of breath and a cough. It will start to become more and more noticeable over time." Steve paused to allow Kim to ask more questions.

"What are the treatment options?"

"There are a few options. Some involve surgery, whereas others need the standard therapy treatment. The worst-case scenario is a lung transplant." Steve started getting some paperwork together for Kim and Austin.

"I hate even asking this but…is… um… is there a time frame?" Kim's voice started shaking.

"If Austin develops other infections it could definitely put him in that category of one year or less. If treatment goes well it could help, but this is a chronic disease, and Austin will have to deal with it for a long time." The expression on Steve's face gave the impression that he knew more than he was saying.

"Just give me a number…please." Kim could hardly keep from crying.

Steve uttered the words: "two years or less." Austin felt faint…*He only had two years to live?*

"I'm sorry. Here's some information about treatment options along with my number so you can reach me at any time. Again, I truly am sorry. There are lots of cases where patients can continue living a mostly normal life." Steve opened the door that led into the hallway.

He followed Austin and Kim to the front desk where he helped make their next appointment. Kim and Austin walked out of the clinic in shock. On the way home Kim pulled through the *Chick-Fil-A* drive-through and ordered them both chocolate milkshakes to help lighten the mood.

"Mom, it's gonna be alright. I promise to fight this as hard as I can. I might not be able to run anymore, but the only thing that matters is that I have you, dad, and Jesus." Austin took a long sip of his chocolate milkshake.

Kim tried not to let Austin see her "proud mom" tears, "I know you'll fight. Your dad and I will be with you every step of the way. We'll get through this together."

↠↠↠

A warm breeze swept through the parking lot while Austin and his parents walked towards church. It was sunny out and the birds were chirping. The parking lot was half full, but cars continued to flow into the empty spots.

Once inside, Austin headed to his seat in the front row while his parents talked to some friends in the atrium. The sanctuary was more empty than it was full. Austin watched as people came to sit down. Occasionally someone he knew would wave or come and say hi, then fifteen minutes later the worship team came out.

Austin enjoyed the music, but not nearly as much as he enjoyed the sermon. After singing two or three songs and taking communion, Pastor Anderson came out onto the stage. Austin held his breath for a minute, taking in every detail.

Pastor Anderson cleared his throat and started the sermon with a prayer, "Father, I ask that you would open our hearts and minds to receive your word today, Amen." He immediately jumped into his sermon. "David wrote many of the Psalms which we find in the Old Testament. He was a king whose subjects affectionately referred to as 'a man after God's own heart.' Christians constantly look to the words he wrote for inspiration." Pastor Anderson took a few steps across the stage and continued. "But, I think we forget that David started as a humble shepherd boy with no plans of becoming a king, oftentimes we see God work like that. He takes a humble nobody from nowhere and uses them to accomplish something great. David wasn't perfect, actually, he was quite the opposite. His life was stained by lies and affairs, but that didn't stop God from using him. So, don't let it stop you. Regardless of your past, God can use you."

John continued to preach about David's time as a young shepherd boy. Austin wrote down as many notes as he could in a notebook he'd brought with him. Once the sermon ended, the worship team came back out and played another song.

02

"Ellie, I'm going to head home now. Do you need anything?" John stepped into his assistant's office.

"I'm good. I'm almost done here, I'll see you tomorrow." Ellie stood up from her desk.

John walked out to his car, which sat alone in the empty parking lot. He turned on a '90s rock playlist to occupy him on his drive home. His house was out towards the country on a little less than three acres of land. His three kids, all girls, were either in college or living on their own.

He pulled into the long, gravel driveway that led to the house. He could see his wife Bree through the kitchen window cooking something for dinner. John walked through the garage door and found Bree.

"Hey, how's your day going?" John grabbed a handful of grapes from the fridge and popped them into his mouth.

"It's going good now that you're here." Bree smiled up at John. "How was church today? You preached on David, right"

"Yeah, it was good. I just don't know what to preach about next week. I'm supposed to have this planned out months in advance, but…" Embarrassment flooded his face. He had a congregation of over 15,000 people looking to him for guidance, and he didn't know what to say.

"You'll figure it out, you always do." Bree started to make a salad to go with their dinner.

"I hope so." John muttered under his breath.

John and Bree shared a quiet dinner and watched some TV before going to bed. When the two had gotten married, John made it a habit of praying out loud for him and Bree every night. But, over the past few weeks, he hadn't done it once. Bree hadn't said anything, although she did wonder why.

They read for a little bit before John kissed Bree on the cheek, said goodnight, and turned off the lights. Bree didn't feel neglected by John, she just felt sorry for him. He'd been different lately, and she could only try to be supportive. It couldn't be easy to be the pastor of one of the largest churches in the state, maybe even the country.

When John went to work the next morning he stopped by Ellie's office before heading to his own.

"Goodmorning, I was planning on taking care of the mountain of emails sitting on my computer, and then I have some other work to do. Is that okay with you?" John sat down in a chair across from Ellie.

"That would be fine except you have three meetings before 2:30."

"When did those get scheduled? I don't have them on my calendar, I don't have time for that." John's tone began to rise, but he tried to keep it under control.

"You have a meeting with the elders, a meeting with the organization we are partnering with to raise money, and umm…" Ellie glanced at her computer to see what John's other meeting was. "Oh, right, a meeting with the pastors at our other campuses."

"Are you sure all of those are today? They aren't on my schedule. I'm not going to have any time to respond to all those emails." John was clearly upset with the current course of the day.

"Yes, I'm sure. Maybe you're looking at the wrong month on your calendar. You know what, I'll respond to all of the emails that I can."

This seemed to calm John down a bit, "Thanks, I should probably get going to that meeting."

He walked out trying to compose himself for his first meeting. The elders were already sitting in the conference room. They greeted John as he walked in and found a seat next to one of the younger elders. The meeting was fairly boring and mostly routine. Their conversation covered that month’s events, finances, and upcoming sermon series.

John left the meeting feeling more tired than he had when he woke up. He sent Ellie a quick text asking her to get him a coffee. He quickly sent another text telling her to get herself something too. Sometimes he felt like he overworked her, but it was her job.

She brought him his coffee right before his second meeting started, “I got through some emails and added the rest of this month’s meetings to your calendar, so there shouldn’t be any more confusion.”

“Thanks, I appreciate it. I’ve got to run to my second meeting.” John took a sip of his coffee before lightly jogging towards his next meeting.

The church was partnering with an organization that helped terminally ill people. John had to meet with them to go over the numbers, and so he could get to know the organization heads better. During the meeting, John met the chairman and they talked about the different stories that he'd witnessed.

"I still remember this one woman who was fighting a treacherous battle with cancer." He paused for a moment, "She had so many people praying for her, fighting with her… I thought she would recover, but she left to be with her Heavenly Father."

A question popped into John's head, "What did you do to help?"

"We offered the family any help they needed after she passed, and while she was still alive we found ways to help the kids stay on track in school. That sort of thing."

"And the money we help raise will go towards that?" John wanted to be able to have awareness about what the church was supporting.

"Yes, the money that you raise will specifically go to help children." The chairman fingered his ornate, gold wedding ring.

"Thanks for chatting with me. I have another meeting to get to, so I'll see you later."

His last meeting went by quickly, leaving him time to work on his sermon and answer some emails. While he was working he got a text from his mentor pastor friend. He'd asked John how things were going and told him he would be in town this week. John replied with a simple: "I'm doing fine, you should come to see me preach this weekend."

His friend said he'd be there on Sunday. John felt more pressure to make sure his sermon was good. People would constantly tell him how a sermon he gave changed their lives. He would almost always reply by saying, "My sermon didn't change your life, God did. I was merely the messenger."

It's what felt right as a reply, but John felt honored to know that his words could be that impactful. After mulling over several topics for his sermon he settled on Abraham sacrificing Issac. Abraham's devotion to God and God's provision of a ram in Issac's place was moving to say the least. Sometimes a sermon would come to John quickly, other times he would have to spend hours thinking and researching before it came together.

Two hours into working he'd gotten the first half of the message worked out. It was almost 5:30, so he decided to take a break until tomorrow. Before leaving he went to see Ellie.

"Hey, I'm heading home, but I wanted to apologize…" This caused Ellie to look up from her work and focus her attention on John. "This morning, I got upset at you for something that wasn't your fault. So… I'm sorry."

Ellie looked slightly surprised, but she smiled at John, "I forgive you. Get some rest tonight, I'll see you tomorrow."

John thanked her and left to go home. Bree had already prepared dinner so they ate right after John arrived. Midway through the meal, John got a call from the church. An elderly member had just taken a turn for the worse. The family had called and asked John to come to visit them.

“Honey, I should go. You could come with me though.” John frowned, he didn't want to go to the hospital tonight.

“I think I’ll just stay here.” Bree pushed her plate forward hinting that she’d lost her appetite.

“I’m sorry, I hate to leave you…”

“Just go…” Bree sounded tired.

John started to say something, but the words didn’t come. He kissed Bree then walked out the door to his car. On his way to the hospital, he said a silent prayer asking God why being a pastor was so much harder than he’d thought it would be. His wife was left sitting at home by herself because he’d followed God’s calling. He would preach about accepting God’s calling in life, and realizing that it won’t always be easy when he couldn’t even apply it to his own life.

He found a parking spot near the front of the hospital. Inside, a receptionist directed him to the third floor. Once he got to the third floor he couldn’t remember the room number, but a nurse standing nearby saw his confused expression and asked him if he was lost. John explained the situation and the nurse was able to help him find the room.

Two people were sitting in chairs across from the bed where a sleeping man lay. John cleared his throat to get the couple's attention.

"Pastor Anderson, come in." The husband motioned for him to enter the room. "I'm Matt, that's my wife's dad, Elias." Matt pointed to the man lying in the bed.

"I'm Jen." Matt's wife spoke softly. It was obvious that she'd been crying most of the day. "Thanks for coming to visit us. Dad loves to watch you preach. He's been a member of Westeast since the beginning."

"That's great to hear." Internally John was shuddering at the whole conversation. One of his biggest pet peeves was when people talked about how long they attended Weasteast or any church for that matter.

The three talked for a few minutes. John occasionally glanced at Elias who was peacefully sleeping with no idea how his current state was affecting those around him.

"Would you like me to pray for him…and you?" Whenever John was called to a hospital meeting like this, the customary thing to do was offer to pray.

"We would love that, thank you." Jen slipped her hand into Matt's and bowed her head.

"Father, It can be hard to understand why people get sick, but it's important to remember that you have a plan for us. Jen and Matt are struggling right now, please comfort them as they wrestle with this situation. And I ask that you would heal Elias whether it be here on earth or in heaven… Amen."

Jen and Matt thanked John for taking the time to come to see them. John walked down the hall towards the elevator when he heard a long beep and a short female scream-cry from the room he'd just been in.

John hung his head to hide the tears that clouded his vision as he took the elevator down to the parking lot. This was the worst part about his job, he hated funerals and late-night hospital visits that never turned out good.

When he got home Bree was already laying in bed.

"How'd it go?" She asked.

"I talked to them, we prayed, and on my way out I heard the heart monitor let out one of those long beeps… and the scream of grief that followed." John put on a pair of pajama shorts before laying down next to Bree.

"Oh John, I'm so sorry. Do we know the people?" Bree cuddled up next to John.

"I've seen them before. I think I talked to them once for a few minutes after service." John's expression was hard and sullen.

Bree's heart melted for John, the two lay in the quiet darkness but neither of them found sleep. Nights like this didn't happen on a regular basis, but when they did happen it turned the mood sour. It took John three hours of fighting his thoughts to fall asleep, but he still tossed and turned all night.

03

"Mom? Can we go out?" Austin roamed through the house looking for his mom.

He found her standing in the kitchen making a cup of coffee, "Sure, we can go somewhere. what were you thinking?"

"Definitely *Starbucks*." Austin started to envision himself drinking a caramel frappuccino.

Kim laughed, "Let's leave in five minutes."

Austin ordered a venti caramel frappuccino and found a seat while his mom waited for the drinks. Soft jazz played over the sound of people ordering and the baristas making drinks.

"Does dad have work tomorrow?" Austin took a sip of his drink.

"Yeah, he has to work the rest of the week." Kim watched Austin as he slurped up the rest of his frappuccino. "Are you ready to go?"

"Yeah, you know… I'm almost sixteen, and I should probably start practicing driving. Maybe I could drive around the parking lot a little bit?" Austin threw his empty cup in the trash.

"Oh… I don't know. How 'bout you wait for your dad." Kim wasn't prepared for Austin to start driving.

"Okay."

When they got home Austin snuck up to his room and put on his running clothes. He knew his mom wouldn't want him running, but the weather was too good to pass up. Austin tried to get out the front door unseen, but Kim heard him open the door.

"Austin, where are you going?" Kim had a round hamper full of laundry under her arm.

"Uhhh." Austin looked up as if the answer was written on the ceiling, "I'm going for a quick…jog."

"A quick jog?"

Austin bent down to "tie" his shoe, or avoid eye contact with his mom, "Yup, I'll be back before you know it."

Kim let out a sigh, "You shouldn't go for a run. What if something happens."

"If I get tired I can come back home. I promise I'll be fine." Austin's eyes were full of longing.

"This one time you may go. I'm asking Doctor Davis if this is allowed at your next appointment."

"Okay, I'll be back soon." Austin walked out the front door and started jogging towards the corner.

His country music playlist was blasting through his *Airpods.* A little less than half-a-mile into the run, Austin started running out of breath. At one point he had to stop in the middle of the sidewalk to keep from falling over. His chest was tighter than it'd ever been before, and he could barely breathe.

He tried to call for help, but the words wouldn't come. A minute later he saw someone frantically running down the sidewalk.

"Austin? Austin?!!?" Kim ran up to Austin, who was still sitting on the sidewalk. "Are you okay? What happened?"

"I…can't…breathe." Austin gasped for air after each word.

"Can you stand up?" Kim tried to help Austin stand, but his legs were too wobbly to hold him up.

Instead of trying to get Austin to stand up, Kim sat down next to him and wrapped him in a hug. His face was red and streaked with tears, but his breathing was starting to calm down.

"Come on, let's get you home." Kim was able to get Austin standing after helping him drink some water.

She acted as his crutch as they walked back home. Kim helped Austin onto the couch before she grabbed her phone and punched in the numbers to call Doctor Davis' office.

"Hello?... Yes, I'd like to move my son's appointment to your next available opening, please… Thursday at nine? Sounds good, see you then." Kim hung up and sat down next to Austin on the couch.

"I'm sorry, I shouldn't have done that." Guilt engulfed Austin's face.

"It's okay, you need to rest. Is there anything I can get for you?"

"Could you grab my Bible, it should be on my nightstand." Austin took small sips from a glass of ice-cold water.

Kim came back with Austin's leather-bound Bible, "Here you go."

"Thanks." Austin flipped through the pages until he found Jesus' sermon on the mount in Matthew.

It brought him comfort while also challenging him to love people one at a time. Since his diagnosis, Austin had found more peace and encouragement reading the New Testament than he had anything else.

"Mom? How'd you know I needed your help?" Austin's eyes locked with his mom.

"It was just a feeling. I knew you needed help, I don't know how else to explain it." Kim silently thanked the Lord for her son's life.

When Ben got home from work he and Kim went into their room to talk.

"Hey." Ben kissed Kim on the cheek. "How was your day?"

"Awful." Kim curled up on a small leather couch that sat along the wall opposite their bed.

"What happened?" Ben unbuttoned his stiff, blue collared shirt.

"Austin went for a run and almost passed out." There was no denying that Kim had taken Austin's diagnosis harder than anyone in the family, Austin included.

"That sounds… awful. I was thinking that I should take a month off of work." Ben pulled a cotton t-shirt over his head. "I don't want to be sitting at a desk looking at a framed picture of my son when I might not ever get to see him again."

"Treatment won't be cheap, you know that." Kim had already roughly estimated the cost of Austin's treatments and any additional hospital stays.

"I know, but we have some money put away, and my family can help out too." Ben had a great deal of wealth that ran through his family because of good investments that struck big.

"You're right, take the time off." Kim got up. "I think I'll go pick up dinner from somewhere. I'm not in the mood to make anything."

Ben nodded and followed Kim out of their bedroom.

"Austin, I'm going to pick up dinner. Love you." Kim left, leaving Austin and Ben alone.

Ben picked up a book off the coffee table and sat down on a gray loveseat in the living room. Austin was still silently studying the sermon on the mount.

"I… uh have something to tell you." Ben dogeared the corner of the page and set the book back on the table. "I'm taking some time off work to be with you and Mom."

Austin didn't respond at first. "Thanks, Dad, that means a lot."

"Since I'm taking the time off I want to do something with you. Just the two of us. Your mom mentioned driving, but I was thinking about a fishing trip." Ben grinned at the thought of going fishing.

"Sure, I'd love to go fishing. We could go to Green Lake." Austin hadn't been fishing for at least six months so the prospect of the upcoming trip was exciting.

“I’ll start planning that.” Ben tried to read his son’s face, there was a visible joy but an underlying depression lay beneath that.

Austin got up to take a shower. He had left his Bible sitting open on the couch. Ben went over to pick it up and he began to flip through it. He found Austin’s messy handwriting next to multiple verses on every page. Words and phrases were underlined or highlighted. Ben continued flipping through when something fell out from in between two of the pages.

It was a small, folded piece of paper with a paragraph written on it. Ben carefully unfolded

it and read the phrase. His eyes immediately filled with tears. Instead of putting the slip of paper back into the Bible, Ben tucked it into his pocket and left the Bible where he found it.

After Austin finished showering, he added some styling gel to his hair. His mind wandered to the doctor’s appointment that awaited him the next day. Although he loved Doctor Davis, he still hadn’t been able to comprehend that he could have less than two years left to live. His dreams of becoming a pastor would be lost in the wind forever.

He couldn't fathom not starting the family he'd dreamed of since he was little. He would miss out on college, mission trips, vacations, having kids and grandkids. Just thinking about it made him feel sick to his stomach. Austin blocked out the morbid thoughts that were swirling through his mind. Instead, he said a prayer to God asking Him to help him live in the moment.

Austin heard the slow rumble of the garage door opening. His mom was home with dinner. As he walked downstairs the smell of Chinese takeout filled the air. Kim and Ben were already sitting at the kitchen table with food on their plates. Austin sat down in between his mom and dad.

Ben picked up his chopsticks and almost stuffed a large bite of noodles in his mouth before Austin stopped him.

"Dad, can we bless the meal first?" Austin gave his dad a mock-judgmental look.

Ben set his chopsticks down and nodded.

"Jesus, thank you for giving us a warm meal to eat. Please help us to enjoy it together as a family. Amen." Austin looked at Ben for approval.

"Thanks for that." An awkward silence followed Ben's comment.

Kim tried to break the invisible tension that had taken over the family's dinner. "Did you and Austin decide what you want to do together now that you have some time off?"

"Yeah, we're going to go fishing." Austin was already looking forward to the trip because it gave him something to be excited about.

"I made a little plan. I was thinking on Saturday morning me and Austin will have a nice breakfast at *Cracker Barrel* and then head out to Green Lake for the rest of the day." Ben scooped a few spoonfuls of white rice onto his plate.

"That sounds good as long as you two get back at a decent time. Austin won't want to miss church." Kim used her chopsticks to pick up a piece of sweet and sour chicken.

“True. I haven’t missed a single sermon this year. I don’t want to break my streak.”

The family finished their meal along with a lighthearted conversation and hearty laughter. Kim was glad that Austin was happy, she had thought that his diagnosis would send him into a long, dark tunnel where he’d be lost forever. Instead, he seemed livelier than ever, he had a good attitude and spirit about everything.

After dinner, the three decided to watch a movie together. Kim had popped some popcorn and they all settled in on the couch to start a feel-good movie based on a true story. Austin fell asleep halfway through, so Ben turned the TV off and laid a blanket over Austin.

“Goodnight buddy,” Ben whispered, so softly that only he could hear it.

Austin woke up the next morning, surprised to find himself on the couch. The sun shone through the curtains in the living room. Austin could hear his mom cooking in the kitchen. He was still groggy from just waking up. The sound of sizzling bacon beckoned him to the kitchen.

"Morning sleepy head." Kim used metal cooking tongs to flip the bacon.

Austin yawned, "Good morning."

Kim made up a plate heaping with hot breakfast foods. Austin's appointment was at 10:30, and it was already 9:45.

"This looks so good." Austin gazed at the plate that was heaping with scrambled eggs, bacon, breakfast potatoes, and a homemade blueberry muffin.

"Eat up! We need to leave in a few minutes for your appointment." Kim peeled the paper liner off of a blueberry muffin and took a bite out of the top.

Austin inhaled his breakfast and helped himself to seconds. After he finished eating he took a quick shower and got ready to go. When they got to the office Kim chatted with the receptionist until they had to go back to the exam room.

Doctor Davis walked into the room and washed his hands before starting the appointment, "Hello! Are you all doing good?" Steve pulled up Austin's file.

"We're doing as good as can be expected. Austin had a scare the other day." Kim folded her hands in her lap.

"What happened?" Steve turned his swivel stool around until he was facing Austin.

Austin stared at the ground until Kim gently elbowed him, "I went for a run."

Doctor Davis looked at Austin as if to say, "What else happened?"

Austin gave in and the whole story spewed out of him. Sometimes when Austin spilled his guts to someone it felt like a huge weight was lifted from him. This time he felt sick to his stomach.

"Okay, you shouldn't be running. It's better that you did it now rather than later so that we know your new limits." Doctor Davis typed some information into the computer. "After looking over your files and studying the x-rays some more, I think we should start treatment soon."

Steve pulled a blue folder stuffed with papers out of his desk. He handed it to Kim, "This folder has all that you need to know about the treatment. It has the name of the clinic we recommend along with their phone number and website."

Kim opened the folder and flipped through the papers. Austin looked over her shoulder as she looked through the papers.

"I can schedule your first appointment and give them all the information for the treatments if you'd like me to." Steve pulled a pen out of his pocket and clicked the top of it.

"That would be really helpful, thank you." Kim closed the folder and put it in her purse.

"I think that's all for now, if you notice an increase in symptoms I can prescribe something for temporary relief, just give the office a call whenever you need to." Steve stood up to shake hands with

Kim and Austin before showing them to the waiting area.

Kim noticed that Austin was clearly struggling with something, " What's wrong?"

Austin could barely look at Kim because he was trying to hide the tears in his eyes, "Nothing. I'm fine."

Sympathy oozed from Kim's voice, "It's okay to not be okay. If you want to talk about it, I'll listen."

"Thanks, Mom." Austin discretely dabbed his eyes with the back of his hands.

Austin and Kim walked into the living room to be greeted by the smell of homemade chicken pot pie. Ben was in the kitchen with an apron tied around his waist. He had flour smudges on his face and clothes.

"Babe, are you cooking us dinner?" Kim wrapped her arms around Ben's neck.

"I'm trying to," Ben added a dash of salt to the crust he was making.

"It smells amazing. Thanks for putting all of this together." Kim watched as Ben put the crust into a pan and poured the chicken pot pie filling onto it.

Ben stuck the dish into the oven and set a forty-five-minute timer. Austin had set the table before going off to do other things.

"So, how did the appointment go?"

"It went well. Doctor Davis said it's time to start treatment. He made us our first appointment for next week." Kim sat down at the island.

"How'd Austin take it?" The comforting smell of Ben's homemade chicken pot pie was seeping out of the oven.

"Not too well. I think he was crying."

A loud timer beeped and Ben pulled the chicken pot pie out of the oven. The hot steam from the oven filled the kitchen.

"Austin! Dinner is ready!" Kim called up the stairs for Austin.

Ben had set the meal in the center of the table. Kim plopped a heaping spoonful of food onto everyone's plate.

There was silence as the delicious meal was devoured.

"Austin, are you ready to leave first thing in the morning?" Ben scraped what little food was left on his plate onto his fork.

"Yup, I packed a bag and my best lures." Austin planned to catch at least seven fish to beat his record of six.

"Great! Get to bed early and we'll leave at 6:00." Ben collected the family's dishes and set them in the sink.

At 6:00 A.M. the next morning Austin's alarm went off to the tune of the *Pirates of the Caribbean* theme. Austin slowly opened his eyes and said a quick prayer asking God to make the day fishing with his dad the best it could possibly be. The night before Austin had set out his clothes and shoes so that he would be ready to go as soon as he woke up.

Austin quickly threw on his outfit and found a red and black checkered flannel in case it got cold. He hopped on one foot while trying to shove on his tan, leather boots. His backpack was lying on the ground next to his bed. He quickly zipped it up and swung it over his shoulder. Ben had just gotten out of the shower and his hair was still glistening with droplets of water.

"Can I drive?" Austin asked with a convincing grin on his face.

"Nope. The passenger seat is wide open though." Ben smiled in a fun-loving way.

The drive to *Cracker Barrel* was short compared to the hour-long drive that awaited them. Austin and Ben both ordered the same meal. While they waited for the food they perused the gift shop that accompanied every *Cracker Barrel.* Ben found a pastel-colored sweater that he bought for Kim. Austin got a bag of sour gummy worms for the car ride.

When the two got back to the table the food was waiting for them. Ben spread a thick layer of jelly onto his biscuits before popping them into his mouth one at a time.

"Dad, I'm really glad we decided to do this." The waitress came by and refilled Austin's orange juice.

"Me too buddy." Ben took a sip from his hot coffee.

After they had finished eating, Ben left a few dollars on the table for a tip and the two went to pay. The second Austin stepped outside the gorgeous weather hit him in the face.

"The weather is perfect for fishing." Ben unlocked the car as he breathed in the fresh air.

An hour and one bathroom stop later, Ben parked the car in the gravel parking lot that overlooked the lake. There were a few other cars already there, but not enough people to crowd the small beach. Austin opened the trunk and grabbed his backpack full of lures and hooks. Ben carried their fishing poles and his tackle box.

"I think that this is a good spot." Austin pointed to the sandy shore a few feet in front of them.

"We can try it." Ben set down the tackle box before handing Austin his fishing pole.

They had packed a small waterproof *Bluetooth* speaker that they could play music on. Austin had downloaded a couple of country playlists the night before. He hit "shuffle" on one of them and adjusted the volume until only he and his dad could hear it.

Ben stuck a worm onto the end of the hook and then cast into the lake. Austin followed his dad's lead, except he put on his favorite jig before casting. A slow period of waiting followed while they watched for fish and tried to lure them in. Even the slightest ripple in the water caused Austin's heart to jump with anticipation. Finally, he felt resistance on the line and he started to reel in. Ben turned his attention to Austin.

"I got one!" Austin pulled the line in all the way to reveal a fat largemouth bass on the end of his hook.

He gently unhooked the fish and held it up while he smiled for a picture.

"Got it." Ben snapped the picture and then put his phone back into his pocket.

Austin released the fish back into the lake and got his line ready to catch another one. The murky, greenish-blue lake water was peaceful. The occasional gust of wind blew across the glass-like surface and created a domino effect of ripples. Ben and Austin talked and laughed while they waited for a bite.

"Austin," Ben turned to his son, "I think I caught something!" Ben used all of his effort to reel in whatever was waiting on the other end of the line.

A mass of slimy green algae and driftwood hung from the end of Ben's line. Austin tried to suppress his laughter.

"C'mon! It was just a stupid vegetarian fish." Defeated, Ben sank back into his chair.

"Don't worry, there's plenty of fish in the lake. Try one of my lures instead of a worm." Austin offered Ben a bright pink jig with a white feather on the end.

"At this point, I'll try anything." So far, Ben had only caught one small bluegill. He attached the lure to the end of his hook and cast towards the far left side of the shore.

The sun started setting an hour or so later. Ben finally caught a fish that was big enough to be proud of. Austin met his goal of seven fish and he wasn't afraid to rub it in.

"I'd say we had a successful day." Ben picked up his folding chair and followed Austin to the car.

"I'd have to agree." Austin buckled his seatbelt and watched the trees pass as they got farther and farther away from one of the best days Austin had had all summer.

04

"Bye Honey!" John finished off a protein bar that served as his breakfast that morning.

Bree was still getting ready, but John had to get to church an hour before the first service. His sermon this week was closing out their current series and he felt the pressure to make it perfect. John still didn't know how he managed to pull off the past couple of weeks.

The church was eerily empty when John got there. A janitor was cleaning a dark-colored spot on the carpet.

"Morning Pastor." The man tipped his head in John's direction and then returned to his cleaning.

John nodded to the janitor and kept walking toward his office. He saw a sliver of light under Ellie's door, so he knocked. A second later Ellie opened the door.

"Thank goodness you're here." John let out a huge sigh of relief.

“Why? What’s wrong?” Ellie stepped outside of her office and looked down the hallway.

A million thoughts came to John’s head as a response to “what’s wrong” but he couldn’t tell her what was actually going on. If anyone found out that he was slipping as a pastor, thousands of weekly congregants would be devastated… and angry.

“The church felt empty, that's all.” John forced himself to smile.

“Okay,” Ellie wasn’t convinced by John’s faux smile, but she decided to let it go, “I have some papers for you and someone emailed asking to meet with you after the 9:00 service.”

John took the thick stack of papers from Ellie, “Meet with me? Who is it?”

“I’d have to look at the email again. Something about a kid who really looks up to you. What should I tell them?” Ellie sat down at her computer to find the email.

"Tell them to email back during the week. I don't have the time to talk to a kid today." John didn't think twice about what he was saying.

"Are you sure? I doubt it would take that long." There was hesitancy and a hint of shock in Ellie's voice.

"They probably just want me to sign one of my books. I'll make it happen, just not today." John shrugged off Ellie's hesitancy, "I have to drop this stuff off in my office and then go get ready for the first service."

After John set his stuff down in his office, he sped walked to the sanctuary. A few of the tech people were setting up behind the stage while the worship team finished warming up. John pulled up his sermon on the little, black iPad he used for reference while he was preaching. He read back through it as a quick refresher.

↠↠↠

"Pastor Anderson, you're almost on." One of the tech workers, Larry, tapped John on the back. He'd been at the church since it was founded and was one of John's favorite people to be around. They'd done countless Bible studies together and Larry had been a great friend over the years.

John walked to the side entrance of the stage, "How have you been?"

"Just fine, thanks for asking. I've been praying for you lately." Larry smiled at John.

"That's very kind of you. We should talk more sometime this week. Maybe we could grab some lunch on Wednesday." John watched the stage for his cue to enter.

"I'd like that. Just shoot me a text." Larry gripped John's shoulder in a supportive way.

The lead singer of the worship team hit the last note on the closing song and John stepped out onto the stage. He zipped right through all of his points and closed out the sermon with a prayer. When the lights went down John slipped backstage as the band came out for another song.

Two services later John was drained and ready to go home. He had promised to take Bree out for a classy Italian dinner and the reservations were for tonight. John was looking forward to some alone time with his wife because it seemed like such a rarity lately.

Bree was reading a book on the couch when John got home.

"Hey babe, church was good today, I liked your sermon." Bree dog-eared the page in her book before closing it.

"Thanks, are you ready to go to dinner?" John untied his dress shoes and put them in the quaintly decorated mudroom.

"Yeah, I just need to grab my purse."

"Okay, I'll get dressed really quick and meet you in the car." John wrapped his arms around Bree's waist, then he slowly kissed her.

"Go get changed." Bree laughed in a carefree, playful manner.

John changed into his dinner attire and drove to the restaurant. The parking lot was full, so John found a valet and handed the kiosk worker the keys. John grabbed Bree's hand as they walked to the entrance. It was dark outside, but little, warm glowing lights lined the exterior of the restaurant, illuminating the surrounding area.

"This is so romantic." Bree smiled up at her husband.

"It's nice to get away from work for a while and focus solely on you." John held open the door for his wife and followed her inside.

The woman at the front grabbed two menus and led them to their table. John continued in his chivalrous acts by pulling out Bree's chair for her.

"What are you going to get?" John was looking at the different appetizers they were offering that day.

"I'm going to try the Pesto Primavera." Bree set her menu down and took a small sip from her iced tea.

"That sounds delicious." John looked at his menu, still deciding what to get.

A waitress stopped by the table and took their orders. A couple of minutes later she delivered a wooden board with a loaf of soft, warm Italian bread sitting on top.

"Could we have some butter for the bread?" John stopped the waitress before she had a chance to walk away.

"Of course, I'll have that right out."

The soft glow of the lights illuminated the cozy booth that John and Bree sat in. Waiters could be seen going from table to table like bees pollinating flowers on a hot summer afternoon in July.

"I don't know if I've ever seen the restaurant this busy." John cut a slice of bread off the loaf, "Do you want some?" He looked up at Bree before setting the knife down.

"Not right now, thanks though." Bree's voice sounded distant and distracted.

Before she even said anything, John knew exactly what was bothering her, "They're fine, they always are. We can call them after dinner if that would make you feel better."

"I know. I just miss having the kids around. I guess that's a part of life though." Sentimentality took over any other emotion Bree was feeling.

"Our kids grew up to have just as big of a heart as you do, which is how I know that they miss you too." John reached across the table and gently took Bree's hand into his own.

"I love you." Bree smiled knowingly at her husband.

The waitress brought out two plates of steaming hot food and set them in front of John and Bree, "Does everything look okay?"

"Yes, it looks amazing." John glanced at the waitress, but his gaze was fixed on his dinner.

Both John and Bree stopped talking for a few minutes while they focused on eating their food. A tall, shadowy figure blocked part of John's peripheral vision. He looked up and saw a man standing at their table.

"Hey! John, it is you, I couldn't tell from the entrance." The man paused to catch his breath. "My name is Mark, I go to Westeast and I wanted to introduce myself."

John internally screamed for the man to leave him alone, but he put on a smile, "Nice to meet you Mark, is there something I can do for you?"

"Other than being the best pastor? No, I just wanted to say hi." A wide smile spread across Mark's face and revealed shiny, white teeth.

"I'm glad that you think of me like that. Enjoy your dinner." John tried to wrap the conversation up.

Mark took the hint and waved goodbye to John as he walked over to his table. John let his head fall into his hands. Bree was silent, waiting for John to say something about the encounter. She was used to people coming up to John and praising him, or hating him. Either way, it had happened enough times for her to know that it was just a part of being married to the pastor of the biggest church in the state.

"Bree… I'm sorry." John couldn't bear to make eye contact with her. "Let's leave, if you're ready."

"It's okay, don't apologize because it isn't your fault." She looked at John lovingly without a hint of frustration.

John stared deeply into Bree's ocean blue eyes, "How… How can you love me even when random people come up to us in the middle of a dinner that was supposed to be special?"

"John Edward Anderson, I didn't marry you because you were the pastor of a megachurch. I married you because you were the pastor of a little baptist church in the middle of nowhere." Bree paused to let her words sink in, "You becoming a pastor of a huge church has been a part of our story, but I wouldn't have it any other way."

John chuckled softly to himself as he reminisced back to the days when he was fresh out of seminary and pastoring a church with a congregation of around seventy people. Never in his wildest dreams would he have pictured himself where he was today, "Thank you for continuing to love me throughout this journey. I couldn't do this without you."

"I know." Bree whispered jokingly.

The waitress stopped by the table and set the bill down. John picked it up and stuck a matte black credit card in front of the receipt without bothering to look at the price. He wrapped his arm around Bree's shoulder as they walked toward the car. For the first time in a long time, John was smiling a genuine smile because he had been reminded that Bree's love for him was unconditional. Bree slowly leaned her head onto John's shoulder and pointed to the sunset that was streaked with yellow, orange, and pink.

05

Soft piano music filled the room. Austin took a deep breath in and looked up to his mom and dad who were standing next to him. His first treatment had just started and he felt like crying, but he knew that he had to stay strong for his mom.

"Austin, do you want to hold my hand?" Kim knelt down so she was on his level.

"No, I'm fine." He drew up a faux smile to try and convince his mom he was going to be okay.

Kim didn't say anything, she simply closed her eyes in order to keep the tears from streaming down her face.

"Excuse me Doc, how much longer will the treatment take?" Ben got the attention of the attending doctor who had just entered the room.

She picked up a dull-colored monitor sitting near the bed that Austin was laying on. "The treatment has just under five minutes left."

Five minutes later a consistent beeping noise came from Austin's monitor, alerting a nurse that his treatment had ended. She detached all of the equipment from him and walked the family back to the waiting area. Kim went to the front desk to check out and schedule Austin's next appointment.

"How are you feeling?" Ben watched his son slowly sit down in one of the waiting room chairs.

"A bit dizzy I guess. Tired." All of the color had been sucked out of Austin's face and his body was limp from exhaustion.

Ben's heart hurt deeply for his son. It seemed like it was only yesterday that they had been laughing together on the lake and nothing was different than before. Now all that remained was a young boy who could barely talk, let alone laugh.

"Take my arm." Ben stretched out his arm in Austin's direction. "I'll walk you to the car."

Austin grabbed onto Ben's arm without hesitation. They walked to the car together, and Kim followed closely behind not noticing how the life had been sucked out of Austin. She had just received a concerning text from her mom and turned her attention to that instead of what was right in front of her.

Ben helped Austin into the backseat of the car and he immediately fell asleep.

"Kim, is this normal?" Concern checkered Ben's face.

"Huh?" Kim still had her eyes glued to her phone, almost as if she was in a trance.

"Look at your son!" Tears clouded Ben's vision. Kim's oblivion to Austin struck up anger in him. "He's dying… and there is nothing… NOTHING I can do about it!"

Ben merged onto the expressway and sped up the car.

"Babe, stop. Slow down." Kim turned around to look at Austin. She gasped when she saw the color of his skin.

Ben had recollected himself and was starting to slow down. "Somethings wrong with him."

"I'll call Doctor Davis and see if there is anything we can do. It might just be a side effect of the treatment." Kim put the phone up to her ear and after three or four dial tones someone picked up.

"Doctor? Hi, this is Kim."

Steve spoke from the other end of the call. "How can I help you?"

"It's Austin. He's not well." Kim turned to look at Austin again and it made her shudder. His usual smile had been replaced with a blank stare, almost as if he was a corpse."There's a sickly, pale glow to his skin and sweat dripping down his face. He's asleep right now."

"It's normal to see those kinds of symptoms after the first treatment, but if it continues to get worse please call me back."

"Thank you Doctor." She hung up the phone and turned to Ben.

"Nothing?" He checked the rearview mirror before getting on the exit ramp.

"He said it's normal for the first treatment to have side effects." Kim looked back at Austin who was peacefully sleeping. "If he's still not doing well in a few days we should bring him in."

Ben pulled the car into the driveway. "Should I wake him?"

"No, we can carry him in." Kim got out of the car and opened Austin's door.

Ben came around on the other side and swept Austin into his loving arms. Kim held open the door for Ben. He set Austin onto the couch and put a throw pillow under his head.

"I'll go grab a blanket." Kim went into the laundry room to find a clean blanket.

Ben sat down at the kitchen table and pulled a piece of paper out of his pocket. Ever since he found it in Austin's Bible he'd been carrying it around everywhere. He carefully unfolded it and read what it said for the one-hundredth time. The handwritten note held words that made Ben cry every time he read them. "*Death, where is your sting? Grave, where is your victory?*" It was those ten words tucked between the pages of Revelation that showed Ben that his son knew he was sick and it would only get worse. But, it was the hope behind those words that allowed Ben to feel at peace because he knew Austin wasn't letting death win.

Kim came into the room carrying a blanket. "Are you okay?"

"Yeah, I'm fine." Ben sat up straighter and swallowed all of his emotions.

Austin slept through the night and woke up around noon the next day. Kim had prepared another feast for breakfast. A tall stack of blueberry pancakes doused in maple syrup sat at Austin's place.

"Mom." Austin sleepily called for his mom to come into the living room.

At the sound of Austin's voice, Kim immediately put her phone down and hurried into the living room. "How are you feeling baby?"

"A lot better. I'm kind of hungry." He slowly sat up on the couch and tried to stand, but couldn't.

"Just stay there, I'll bring you some breakfast." Kim scurried back to the kitchen and grabbed Austin's food. "Here, eat this."

"Thanks. It feels like lunchtime though." Austin slowly took a bite of the pancake sitting on the top of the stack.

"That's because it is lunchtime." Kim handed Austin a napkin. "You've been asleep for a long time. Your dad and I were starting to get worried."

Austin started to eat a little faster as Kim filled him in on what had happened in the last twenty-four hours. The color and life had come back to his face while he was asleep. Kim had checked in on him every few hours to make sure that he was still breathing. The effects of the treatment had made her and Ben question if it was really worth it.

"Mom, these pancakes are amazing. I think you missed your calling as a chef." Austin had polished off the last pancake in three minutes.

"If I had become a chef I wouldn't be able to be your mom." She had majored in culinary arts and had always dreamt of being the head chef of a restaurant in New York City.

"You know, my birthday is right around the corner. Maybe since it's my 16th we could throw a huge party. Most of my friends will be back from vacation since school starts in a few weeks."

"I'm sure we can make something happen." Kim took Austin's empty plate and headed back to the kitchen.

Austin got off the couch and carefully walked up the stairs to his room. Kim had come in and cleaned because the bed was made and the floor was spotless. Austin spotted his Bible sitting on his desk. He grabbed it and hopped into bed. His bookmark was in Luke 2, but Austin remembered reading something in Revelation after his diagnosis that he'd wanted to study deeper. He'd even written a note and stuck it in the Bible to mark his place. When he flipped through the pages to find it, he couldn't.

Perplexed, Austin shut the Bible and went into his bathroom. He hadn't showered in a couple of days and taking a lengthy hot shower always helped him clear his mind. Austin turned the water on and got ready to get in. The hot water burned his scalp at first, but after a few seconds, he got used to the temperature. With his eyes closed and the hot water rolling down his skin, Austin thanked God that he'd gotten through his first treatment.

The last thing Austin remembered from the treatment was falling asleep in the car. He never wanted to go through that again, but the doctor told him that it may be his only chance of surviving. At least he had his birthday party to look forward to. Austin shut off the water and wrapped himself in his dry towel.

He put on clean clothes and went back downstairs to see what his parents were up to. They were sitting on the couch together, talking.

"What's up?" Austin sat down in the oversized, cushioned chair across from them.

"We were talking about your big party." Ben took a sip from the glass of water in his hand. "What theme were you thinking?"

"Probably just classic party-themed. Colorful balloons and streamers, that kind of thing." Austin hadn't given much thought to the theme of the party.

"How many people did you want to invite?" Kim grabbed a blank notebook that was sitting on the table and started writing down the details of the party.

"I want to invite about thirty people, most from school, some family friends, and you and Dad can invite whoever you want." He watched as Kim scribbled everything down into the notebook. "Oh, I also wanted to have the party in a week. I can make the invitations today and send them out as an E-vite."

Ben had to keep himself from spewing his water everywhere, "A week?!? That's not a lot of time."

"It's plenty of time, don't worry I'll work to make it happen." Austin had a glint of unstoppable determination in his eyes.

Ben looked at Kim with concern, but she sided with Austin, "This is what he wants, we can sacrifice some time to throw the biggest 16th birthday bash ever…because it could be the last birthday he gets."

"I don't know about 'ever,' but we can probably make it happen." Ben was reluctant to make such a big commitment, but because it was for his son he was willing to compromise.

"Sweet!" Austin pumped his fist in the air. "I'll start working on the invites right now."

His enthusiasm filled Kim's soul with joy. Even if he was terminally ill, he still had the spirit of the little boy Kim and Ben had raised. Austin went back upstairs to work on the invitations.

"He's really happy. If I was him right now there is no way that I would be as happy as he is." Kim let Ben wrap his arm around her shoulder in a loving way.

"I feel like we have to give him the world because he might not live long enough to see it." Ben's gaze was fixed on a non-existent point somewhere in the distance.

"He has a chance. If he can stay healthy and…" Kim was interrupted by a loud cough from upstairs. "Knock on wood… I'll go see if he's alright." She got up from the couch and headed to Austin's room.

Kim pushed open the door to find Austin sitting on his bed typing on his laptop. "I heard you coughing, are you okay?"

"I'm fine, I think I just swallowed too much air or something." Austin clacked away on the keys. "I finished the invitations. I'm about to email them out. Wanna see?"

Kim walked to the bed and looked over Austin's shoulder. "Those look really nice. I'm going to go to *Party City* tomorrow to get some decorations, could you please come with me?"

"Of course." Austin hit send on the email and shut his laptop.

"We need to think about what kind of food you want to have." Kim sat down on the edge of Austin's bed.

"How 'bout an *Olive Garden* family-style type thing." Italian food was his favorite, so it seemed fitting that he would have it at his party.

"I'll have your dad look into that."

Kim headed back down the stairs. Austin shut the door behind her and sat back down on his bed. The comforter sunk in under his weight. He leaned over to check the time on a portable alarm clock that he kept on his nightstand. The tiny flashing red numbers read 8:30 P.M. Austin hadn't realized how late it'd gotten.

He pulled out his Bible and flipped through the pages until he found his place. After reading a couple of chapters Austin set the Bible on his bookshelf and started to say a prayer before he turned in for the night.

"Heavenly Father, How was your day? My day was pretty good, I was thankful for the idea of having a party but something has been bugging me all day." Austin looked across the room to make sure his door was shut before continuing. "I have a question... Why me? Why do I have to be so sick that I have to die? It's not fair, the Bible says that you have a plan for me and that you love me but how is it love if I'm dying?" Tears streaked Austin's face as he cried out to God.

He heard a sound outside his door, so he quickly pulled the covers over himself and turned his light off. "I know that you love me…I'll try to trust you, but I'm going to need some help." Austin shut his eyes and drifted off to sleep.

Kim was already laying in bed when Ben entered their bedroom. "Did you see Austin?"

"No… I heard him though." Ben seemed distant as he laid down next to Kim.

"Heard him? I don't understand." Kim turned onto her side so that she was facing Ben. When she looked into Ben's eyes she saw a deep hurt that she'd only seen a few times. "Babe, are you okay?"

"I'm fine um…just tired." Ben was flat on his back, his eyes fixed on the ceiling fan. The room was silent for a few moments. "It's Austin, but I don't want to talk about it right now."

"Well, whenever you want to talk about it, I'll listen." Kim waited for a couple of seconds before turning off her nightstand light.

The party snuck up quicker than anyone had anticipated. Ben had called the caterer and gotten the food. Kim and Austin had decorated the whole house and come up with multiple party games to play. Everything was silently sitting in place while they waited for the guests to arrive. Bright colored balloons lined the walls, streamers had been strung across the ceiling, and a huge chocolate birthday cake sat in the center of the kitchen table.

Austin was anxiously waiting for the first guest to ring the doorbell. He had been watching the front window like a hawk for the past thirty minutes. Finally, a car pulled up into the driveway and someone holding a bright red gift bag stepped out. Austin sprinted to the door and opened it before they even had a chance to knock.

"Hey Austin, happy birthday!" A girl around Austin's age greeted him from across the porch.

"Hey, it's good to see you Anna, please come in!" Austin ushered her into the house and Kim took the gift and started a pile in front of the fireplace.

After the first guest arrived there was a constant flow of people until everyone had arrived. The house was full of chatter and people squeezing past each other to get a cup of soda or a plate of food. Austin spent the majoirty of the party talking to his best friend James..

Kim walked into the room and stood on a stool, "Everyone!" she waved her arms to get everybody's attention. "I think it's time to have some cake!"

Slowly, all the guests trickled into the kitchen to sing happy birthday to Austin. Kim had Austin sit at the table so that everyone could see him. Ben brushed his hand over the light switch and the room transformed in the candlelight. One of Austin's friends, who was a singer, led the group in a chorus of happy birthday. As soon as they hit the last note Austin took a large breath in and blew out all sixteen candles on the cake. Everyone clapped and Ben turned the lights back on.

"If you want cake there's enough for everyone, I'll start cutting slices and passing them out. We also have cupcakes if you would prefer that." Kim headed to the table with a cake cutter and a thick stack of paper plates.

People started lining up to get a piece of cake. Austin grabbed a piece for him and James and they snuck into the living room. The two had already covered the topic of summer vacation and the start of school next year, but there was something Austin had avoided bringing up. Most people at the party didn't really know what had been going on with him, and if they did looks of pity crossed their faces when they saw Austin.

Kim poked her head around the corner and told all of the people in the living room they would start opening presents in five minutes.

"James… there's something I have to tell you." Austin avoided eye contact with his friend.

"Dude, what's going on?" James could tell that something was bothering Austin.

"Over the summer I was diagnosed with-" Before Austin could finish his sentence a wave of nausea swept over him.

His face started to lose color ever so subtly. Over the past couple of weeks, this had happened to him a couple of times. Dr. Davis had said it was common after the first treatment to experience symptoms such as nausea and fatigue, but Austin had also developed a nasty cough.

"Are you okay?" James shook Austin's shoulders for a second. When Austin didn't respond James ran into the other room to find Kim. "Mrs. O'Conor, Austin's acting weird."

"Where is he?" Panic engulfed Kim's body as she followed James to the living room.

Austin was sitting on the couch with his head between his knees. When Kim asked him what was wrong he broke out into a coughing fit.

"Ben!" Kim shouted across the house. "Call an ambulance!"

All of the guests stopped what they were doing and rushed into the living room. James tried to get them all back into the kitchen so that Austin could have some space.

"The ambulance is on its way." Ben had just finished talking to the emergency service operator.

"Is he going to be okay?" James felt numb with pain for his friend. They had known each other since they were in Kindergarten. Austin had invited him to church and they'd been friends ever since. James had always thought of Austin as a rock that he could cling onto when the storm of life was too much to bear. Now, James started to imagine how he would keep going without Austin.

"He's going to be fine. I'm assuming he didn't tell you?" Ben sat down next to James.

"No sir, he didn't." James bowed his head in silence.

The fatherly instinct in Ben kicked in and he set his hand on James' knee in a comforting way. Most of the guests from the party quietly snuck out after saying goodbye to Ben or Kim. Those who were still there were some of Austin's closest friends. Wailing ambulance sirens could be heard approaching in the distance.

Austin had come to his senses and was able to talk to Kim, but he looked deathly sick and his body was shaking. The paramedics knocked on the door and Ben hastily went to open it for them. Two burly men lifted Austin onto a stretcher and wheeled him into the back of the ambulance. Kim went with him and Ben planned to get in his car and follow behind. He thanked James and the rest of Austin's friends who had stayed before showing them out and leaving.

Ben found Kim sitting in the waiting area, rapidly tapping her foot against the ground. He sat down next to her and waited a moment before asking if there was any news on what was happening to his son. When he asked, Kim slowly looked up and rested her head on his shoulder.

"They said they're doing everything they can. They are going to run blood tests as soon as possible, but they think that he got an infection or some kind of pneumonia that made the PAP get worse." Kim let a tear slip out of the corner of her eye and roll down her cheek. "I should have taken him to see Doctor Davis the second he started coughing."

"How could you have known? Austin would tell you that God has a plan and there is no amount of regret that can change that." Ben embraced his wife as she quietly sobbed.

The methodical sound of machines beeping and nurses in baby blue scrubs hurrying from place to place filled Kim and Ben's heads within twenty-four hours. They had only been allowed to see Austin once since they had gotten there. He looked much better than he had when he first arrived, but it was obvious that something was wrong with him.

06

"Hey… John, come here for a minute." Ellie called to John from inside her office.

He stood up from his swivel chair and stretched his arms up above his head. "I'll be right there." He walked over to Ellie's cubicle-like office. "What's up?"

"You got another email from those people who wanted to meet you. The guy said it was really important." Ellie scrolled through her computer until she found the email.

"Do you have the books I signed for them?" John sat down on the corner of Ellie's desk.

"Yes, I still need to send them, but they really want to meet with you." Ellie found the box of signed books and taped them up. "I'll run these down to the office so they can mail them out. What should I tell the family?"

"I don't know when I can meet with them. They can try to catch me on a Sunday after service. I think I have a video shoot this weekend if they want to try to meet me after that." John walked to the door and let Ellie slide past him into the hallway. "Also, I have a lunch meeting that I'm about to leave for."

"Okay, are you coming back after?" Ellie tucked the box of books under her arm.

"I doubt it. I'm meeting with a member who is really struggling and it'll probably be a long lunch." John checked his pocket to make sure he had his car keys as he followed Ellie down to the lobby.

John drove the charming lunch bistro with the windows rolled down and the spring breeze blowing through his hair. He didn't know the person he was meeting, but the request had said urgent. He was looking forward to a nice lunch with someone new. Someone leaving the restaurant held the door for John and he stepped inside. There was a short line of people waiting to order at the counter.

John scanned the room for the person he was meeting with. He saw a young man sitting alone towards the back of the restaurant. John approached the man and sat down across from him

"Are you Brent?"

"Yes sir, you're John Anderson." Brent looked like he was a junior in college and the dark circles under his eyes concerned John.

"You asked to meet with someone. What's going on?" John took a sip from a sweet tea that Brent had ordered for him.

"I'm struggling with a lot of things. My girlfriend broke up with me a few weeks ago, I haven't talked to my parents in ages… and I think I have a drinking problem." Brent couldn't bear to look at John, it was the first time he had taken off the mask that he'd been hiding all of his problems behind.

John fixed his eyes on Brent and he could almost see his reflection. Even though he wasn't dealing with the same problems as Brent, he was wearing a mask to cover his problems too.

"I can recommend a program for drinking addicts. I can also recommend a phone call to your parents. Why haven't you talked to them?" John rubbed circles on his temples with his fingers as he thought about what else to do to help Brent.

"I'm embarrassed. They think that I'm successful and that I have a girlfriend and that my life is figured out, but it's just falling apart." Brent's soul slowly started to crumble as he opened up to a man who he only knew from a distance.

John took a long sip from his tea before responding to Brent. "They're believing a lie, and now it's too big to retract. The only way to fix a lie is to tell the truth. Call them, even when you were a kid they were the people who helped you with all your problems and they still are."

Brent nodded, it wasn't the answer he wanted to hear, but it was the answer he knew had been coming. "I'll call my dad on the way home."

John tried to help Brent over the next hour. They talked about what had gone wrong in his relationship and why he'd developed a drinking habit. John prayed for him and they walked out of the restaurant together.

While John drove home, he thought about his conversation with Brent. It was the first time he'd felt like he was actually doing his job in months. Brent's vulnerability opened John's heart to seeing that being honest can create an opportunity for healing. When he pulled into the driveway he made the decision to tell Bree what had been going on with him. She deserved to know anyway.

"Bree, can you come here?" John's stomach was tied up in knots of nervousness.

Bree walked into the room and sat down across from John. "What's wrong? Did something happen at work?"

John simply shook his head. "I need to tell you something that I haven't told anyone, but I should've shared much sooner." He closed his eyes and faced the reality that he was about to reveal everything that he'd been hiding for months. "I'm slipping… I can't find the motivation to write a sermon that I'm proud of, I can't practice what I preach to thousands of people on Sunday morning. I don't have time for anything except for meetings and answering emails… I haven't talked to God in weeks…"

John's words didn't seem to phase Bree. "It seems like you're forgetting the most important thing…"

"What?" John sat up on the couch and stared into his wife's loving eyes.

"God is the missing puzzle piece. This-" Bree waved her arms around. "This isn't about you. When you find God, the rest will fall into place."

"It's like I saw the problem right in front of my face this whole time, but I kept looking past it."

John wiped a tear from his face. "Bree, will you please pray with me?"

"I'd love to." Bree sat down next to John and took hold of his hand before praying for him. After she finished praying she made a suggestion. "If I remember correctly, you're speaking at a conference in Texas in a few weeks. I think you should reach out to your old seminary professor for more guidance."

"That's right, I haven't talked to Doctor Bamford in years. He was one of the best mentors I've ever had." John made a mental note to email him later in the week. "Thanks for listening to me. Even though I feel like a huge weight has been lifted off my shoulders, I still have more work than I care to think about."

"With God, all things are possible. You aren't alone anymore John. You never were." Bree wrapped John in a loving embrace and kissed him.

"How would you feel about preaching this Sunday?" John teased Bree. "I think you'd do better than me."

Bree laughed a laugh that John had heard a million times but never got tired of hearing. They stayed on the couch for a while longer and turned on a movie. Both of them fell asleep before the movie was over. The moonlight shone through the curtains and cast shadows along the living room walls. Both John and Bree slept peacefully through the night.

07

It had been three days since Austin was admitted to the hospital. Doctor Davis had been by once to evaluate the situation, but he was coming back today to talk about the next steps. Austin had spent his time watching John Anderson's old sermons and a few of his favorite movies.

Kim stepped into the room. Austin was laying down on the bed with various machines surrounding him. Every time he breathed in, a raspy sound escaped his lungs and a terrible cough followed each breath he took.

"Doctor Davis is on his way over to talk with you." Kim tried to put on a brave smile for her son. She sat down in one of the nondescript hospital chairs that seemed to be in every room of every medical building.

"Mom, do you think Doctor Davis is a Christian?" Austin had been pondering whether or not the man who could end up saving his life knew his real Savior.

"Umm…honey, I don't know." Austin's question didn't surprise Kim, but it caught her off guard. Somewhere deep down, she had been thinking the same thing since they had met Steve.

Austin wasn't satisfied with his mom's answer, but he had been praying for Doctor Davis a lot since his first appointment. Kim and Austin continued to talk about random topics until Doctor Davis' tall frame filled the doorway.

"Hello. How are you feeling today?" Steve had a sleek, black briefcase dangling at his side. He sat down on the edge of Austin's bed and unclipped the latches that kept it closed. It was filled with Austin's paperwork and the back pouch revealed Steve's laptop.

"I'm feeling the same as I have for the past three days. Not good." Austin tried to stifle a cough, but it only sounded louder than he'd intended.

"It sounds like you're feeling worse." Steve opened his laptop to Austin's file so he had a point of reference. "After our last conversation, I came up with some options. The new x-rays revealed that Austin's lungs are not improving. Your only true shot at making it out of this is a lung transplant."

Doctor Davis' words registered in Austin's head, *"your only true shot..."* A wave of anxiety swept over Austin as Steve continued to talk about the process of getting a lung transplant. Somewhere in the deepest part of Austin's soul, he heard a whisper saying *"My peace I give you. I do not give to you as the world gives. Do not let your heart be troubled and do not be afraid."* Peace overwhelmed the anxiety that had so readily taken over Austin's emotions. Doctor Davis started talking about how they would need to find a match for a lung transplant.

Austin interrupted him. "Excuse me Doctor, how much time will I have until…"

"I was getting there. If the transplant succeeds then you could have up to ten years, maybe even twenty." Steve's tone was optimistic.

"And if it fails?" Austin's voice trailed off into a dark abyss of doubts and fear.

"It won't."

Steve's confidence struck Kim as a little cocky. It was comforting but at the same time, he wasn't the one who was going to perform the surgery. He packed up his briefcase after handing Kim a stack of papers.

"Do you have any other questions before I leave?"

"How long will Austin have to stay here?" Kim looked up at Steve as he headed to the door.

"At least until after the surgery and that all depends on finding a match, which I'm going to start working on that when I get back to the office. Anything else?" Steve was anxious to leave, but he waited.

"No that's it, thank you."

Steve leaned against the wall outside of Austin's room. He was used to seeing patients live in the hospital with life-threatening diseases, but something was different about Austin. Steve closed his eyes and let his briefcase sink to the floor. There was an innocent child dying on the other side of the wall and there was nothing he could do about it except try to smile and deliver the news that they wanted to hear.

Steve let his face fall into his hands and a fat tear landed on the tip of his finger. He quickly swiped it away and walked towards the elevator. He'd seen other doctors crack under the pressure of the job, but this was one patient out of hundreds if not thousands. In a couple of months, Austin would be on his way to recovery and Steve would never see him again. The elevator doors closed behind him and he pushed all thoughts of Austin out of his mind.

↠↠↠

Ben had just gotten back to the hospital after going home to shower and take a nap. He and Kim had been switching places so that Austin wouldn't be left alone, but it was getting tiring and they would have to figure something else out.

Ben pulled out his laptop and opened his email. It had been a week since he'd emailed John's assistant, and he was checking to see if she'd responded. He clicked the refresh button and a plethora of messages popped up. Ben scrolled through until he found one from the secretary. Disappointment filled Ben when he saw her response. She'd said there was no for sure time to meet John.

It made Ben wonder if it was really a good thing if he'd been a member of a church for at least ten years and had only talked to the pastor a handful of times. He'd reached out to see if they could meet John because he knew it would mean the world to Austin, but it seemed impossible to get through.

Ben shut his laptop in frustration. Austin had fallen asleep a half hour ago and his Bible still lay open on his chest. Ben quietly walked over to the hospital bed and carefully picked up the Bible, so he wouldn't wake Austin. Ben sat back down in his chair and laid his baseball cap over his eyes. He dozed off to sleep within minutes.

Austin awoke to a knock on the door. "Come in."

Kim slid open the door. "You have a visitor."

James stepped out from behind Kim and sheepishly waved at Austin. A wide smile stretched across Austin's face at the sight of his friend. Ben woke up from his nap and left the room to give Austin and James a minute alone.

"What's up?" James sat down in the chair that Ben had been napping in.

"Nothing, I'm not allowed to do anything except stay in bed. It's boring. You're the first visitor I've had."

"A lot of the girls at the party were worried about you." James sat up a little taller and prepared himself to do an impression of the girls. "Oh, poor Austin I feel so bad for that poor boy."

"Yeah right." Austin chuckled sarcastically.

"Oh yes, every word of it is true. I promise you." James tried to hold back a fit of laughter, but it was no use.

He and Austin laughed until their stomachs hurt. Austin was beyond grateful for the company. After James left, he would be back to watching old sermons and binge-watching whatever he could find on *Netflix*.

"Hey, before I go… Can I ask a personal question?" James' lightheartedness from earlier had transformed into something more serious.

"Sure." Austin had a million ideas of what James' question could be floating through his head.

"How much longer are you going to be here? School starts in a week and I don't think you can go dressed in a hospital gown."

Relief rushed over Austin because James had not asked the dreaded question. "I'll be here until they can do the lung transplant, and then after that… I don't know."

"Oh… I'll miss you at school." James stood up, his eyes trained on the floor. "Get better soon Austin… Please."

James started to walk out the door but at the last second, he turned around and ran to Austin's bed. He wrapped Austin in a bear hug and then let him go. James walked out of the room without a word. Austin tried to say something but nothing came out except a tear that he quickly brushed away.

Kim came into the room and sat down on the edge of Austin's bed. "How are you feeling?"

"The same as always. Not good." Austin let out a deep cough and wrapped his arms around his chest.

"I'm sorry. Me and your dad aren't going to be able to stay here all the time. Your nurse told us that we are okay to leave and go home, but I want to make sure that's okay with you."

After a moment of thinking, Austin replied. "That's fine. There's no reason for you to stay all the time."

"We're still going to stay with you during the day, but tonight we are going to go home so we can get some rest." Kim ran her fingers through her silky hair.

Ben came to say goodbye to Austin and sooner rather than later, Austin was left alone. The sounds of a busy hospital came to a slow halt as the night crept in. The silence was eerie, but Austin had turned on the TV so that it was softly playing in the background. He didn't realize how much he would miss having his parents around. As Austin fell asleep to the slow hum of the machines that surrounded him, he internally fought with himself. *If he felt totally and utterly alone now, how would his parents feel if he didn't make it?*

Throughout the night a terrible nightmare plagued Austin. In it, he was standing in a stark, white room by himself. There was a door directly across from him and when it opened, two mangled bodies walked into the room. They dripped blood across the floor and started to yell out Austin's name. It took him a minute to realize that the bloody corpses were his parents. Austin started to back away from what used to be his parents, but there was nowhere to go. He felt himself fall to the ground and wrap his arms around his knees as if it would protect him.

Then, in the moment of desperation, he did the only thing he knew to do, he whispered the name of Jesus. Austin woke up with a cold sweat dripping down his forehead. He inhaled sharply and sat up. The clock hanging on the wall across from his bed indicated that it was three in the morning. Austin knew he couldn't fall back asleep, but it was Saturday and there was something he had to do.

He turned the lights on and grabbed a pad of paper that his mom had left on accident. Austin started to write his letter to Pastor Anderson. He wrote how thankful he was for John and the impact that being a part of Westeast had made on him. Towards the end of the letter, Austin decided to write about his nightmare. He wrote down every detail that he could recall. Austin signed the bottom of the letter with his loopy, cursive signature.

↠↠↠

Days went by and Steve still hadn't been able to find a match for the lung transplant. It was a sunny Friday afternoon. Kim was reading a book in Austin's room and Ben was at the house planting flowers.

"Mom, I'm getting kind of hungry." Austin had been watching a documentary about the life of Jesus, but he was getting bored of it.

"Okay, I'm pretty hungry myself. I think I'll go eat in the cafeteria, but I'll bring you back something. What do you want?"

"Whatever looks the best. I'm sick of hospital food." Austin had been eating questionable meals for almost two and a half weeks and he was ready for a change.

"I'll have your dad bring you something good for dinner." Kim dropped her book into her purse. "I'll be back soon!"

She walked down to the hospital cafeteria and grabbed a salad and a fruit cup from one of the grocery store-style refrigerators. There were floor-to-ceiling windows surrounding the seating area. The golden sunshine bathed the tables in warm sunlight. Kim found a table for two and pulled out her book. As she was eating her salad she saw someone with blue scrubs approaching her table.

It was Austin's main nurse, Claire. "Can I sit down?"

"Sure." Kim set her book down and watched as Claire sat down across from her. "What's up?"

"I had a question for you. About Austin." Claire's emerald green eyes danced in the sunlight.

"Yes?" Kim took a bite of her salad.

"I've been a nurse for a couple of years and I've never met anyone as joyful as Austin. Someone so weak yet so strong. Why is that?"

Kim smiled because she knew that Austin wanted to be a light in the darkness, and this showed that he had been. "It's because Austin has

Jesus in his heart. His faith gives him the strength to smile in the suffering."

"I've met lots of Christians before, but I don't get it. If I was in Austin's shoes I would be on the verge of…" Claire didn't finish her sentence but Kim knew what she was going to say.

"You should ask Austin about it. He would love to tell you." Kim took the last bite of her salad. "Anything else you wanted to talk about?"

Claire hesitated, but she chose to talk. "As I said, I've been working here for a few years, and it's getting pretty taxing. I take as many shifts as I can because I have a lot of debt to pay off from student loans and other things. I broke up with my boyfriend because he had a drinking problem. It feels like my life is slowly falling apart."

"I'm sorry. I don't have much advice to offer you, but I would love to invite you to come to church with me and Ben. If you're okay with it I'd be happy to pray with you too." Kim offered a sympathetic smile, however, she was sorry she couldn't offer more.

"I appreciate that, thank you."

Kim prayed for Claire and they kept talking about what had been going wrong in Claire's life. They were able to come up with some things to help her and Claire had agreed to go to church with Kim and Ben.

Austin had gotten tired of waiting for his mom to bring him lunch, so he had called Ben and asked him to pick up something. Ben brought Austin a pizza from an Italian bistro near the hospital.

"I don't know where mom is. She said she was going to bring me lunch, but that was at least an hour ago." Austin finished off his first slice of pizza.

"Maybe she forgot…" Ben sat down in what had become "his chair."

Just as Austin had finished eating his lunch, Kim walked into the room. "Ben, when did you get here?"

"Around twenty-five minutes ago. Where have you been?"

"Oh, I was talking to Austin's nurse, Claire." Kim leaned against the wall. "Sorry for forgetting about your lunch buddy."

"That's okay, dad brought me pizza."

The family spent a couple of minutes talking and laughing as though they were sitting around their kitchen table playing a heated game of *UNO*. After a while, Kim left to run some errands. Ben was answering some emails when a text from his friend Josh came in.

"Hey man! Shawna told me that Austin was in the hospital. I thought we would stop by to say hi to you and Kim and offer Austin some support. When's a good time?"

Ben quickly responded that they could come visit that evening after texting Kim to let her know. Josh immediately responded with a thumbs up.

"Austin, you're going to have some visitors tonight." Ben turned off his phone and focused his attention on Austin.

"Who?" Austin was glad for any company that wasn't his parents or the hospital staff.

"Josh and Shawna. We had lunch with them a few weeks ago."

Austin vaguely remembered eating with them, but he knew who they were nonetheless. Time in the hospital seemed to pass slower than it did anywhere else. What should've felt like a couple of hours felt like an eternity to Austin. The hour hand on the clock moved more sluggishly than the clock in Austin's room at home. It had only been a couple of weeks and Austin had already read through the New Testament of his Bible twice. He'd seen just about everything there was to see on TV.

He was getting restless, and he thought that if he didn't die of lung failure, he would surely die of insanity. Austin had been nagging his parents to ask the nurse if he could go outside in a wheelchair, but his request seemed to slip through the cracks.

Austin cleared his throat to get Ben's attention. "Dad, do you think you could ask the nurse about going outside?"

"Uh… why not?" Ben got a nearby nurse's attention. "Excuse me, ma'am, my son has been stuck inside for weeks. Is there any way we can take him outside?"

"I'll have to see what machines he's currently using and if they can be easily transported, but I'm sure that can be arranged." The nurse started to look at the various medical devices surrounding Austin's bed. "Is now a good time?"

Before Ben had a chance to answer, Austin blurted out an excited "Yes." The nurse laughed and went to get a wheelchair for Austin. When she came back Ben got up to help Austin into the chair.

"Are you comfortable?" The nurse adjusted a tube that was attached to one of Austin's machines.

"Yes, thank you."

Austin signaled for Ben to push him towards the elevators. It felt like the first time in days since Austin had seen anything outside of the four gray walls that made up his new room. Ben wheeled Austin through the automatic opening doors and into the hospital parking lot. The sun instantly warmed Austin's pale skin. There were birds chirping playfully in the distance, and a warm summer breeze rustling through the leaves of the oak trees.

Ben pushed Austin towards a small garden that the hospital maintained in the warm seasons. A multitude of blooming flowers lined the gravel pathway. A giant orange butterfly fluttered past Austin's eyes and into the sea of flowers.

Austin took a moment to breathe in the fresh air. "I want to live outside, the weather is better than perfect."

"You won't have to stay in that stuffy hospital room much longer." Ben parked the wheelchair next to a bench so he could sit down.

"How come?"

"Your mom wanted me to wait to tell you until she was here, but Doctor Davis called and he found a match! The surgery is currently scheduled for a week from tomorrow." The sun illuminated the smile on Ben's face.

"Seriously? Just one week and then I'm out of this gross place?" Austin was practically speechless. He'd started to think that he would be stuck in the hospital forever.

"Dead serious. In one week you'll be on your way to recovery. If things go well you might be able to go to school second semester."

Austin could hardly contain his excitement, after three weeks of waiting, one week seemed like a piece of cake. As Ben pushed Austin back towards the hospital the birds seemed to chirp a little bit louder and the sun seemed just a little bit brighter.

Kim was already inside when Ben wheeled Austin back into his room. "Hey you two! Shawna and Josh are going to be here any minute."

Austin carefully stepped out of the wheelchair once he was close to his bed. His legs felt like Jello as he tried to stand up. He fell back onto the bed, with his legs landing in the air. A joyful laugh escaped from Austin when he landed on the airy duvet cover.

"Are you okay?" Kim tried to sound genuinely concerned, but she was suppressing a laugh.

"I'm fine, that was actually fun."

Ben was helping Austin get situated when Shawna and Josh knocked on the door. Kim got up to hug Shawna. Austin's room felt crowded with four people occupying what little space there was.

"How do you feel Austin?" Josh leaned against the doorframe with his arm wrapped around Shawna's waist.

"Physically, not so great. Mentally, better than I have in weeks. My dad just gave me the news that I'm going to have my lung transplant in a little over a week."

"That's great!" Shawna had been holding a tiny gold gift bag with white tissue paper sticking out of the opening. She handed it to Austin. "Open it."

He gently removed the tissue paper from the top and peered into the bag. There were two items sitting on top of a yellow envelope. Austin pulled out a devotional for teen boys along with a pocket-sized compass that had part of Psalm 37:23 engraved on the top. *"The Lord directs the steps of the godly."* Before opening the envelope Austin thanked Shawna and Josh for the gift

"I'm glad you like it. I picked out the compass as a reminder that God knows the direction you need to go even if it feels like it's the wrong way." Josh had put a lot of thought into what they should get Austin, and he was relieved that Austin liked it.

The unopened envelope was sitting on top of Austin's bed. He picked it up and tore open the flap that held it shut. There was a "get-well-soon" card with a message written on the inside.

"I don't understand..." Austin set the card down and looked up at Josh.

"Shawna and I wanted to tell you how much we are looking forward to getting to see you grow into a young man after your surgery."

"But... what if?" The message about the certantiy of the future felt like someone stabbing a knife through Austin's chest.

Shawna stepped forward. "We have confidence that God will see you through this hard time in your life."

Before Austin could respond Kim stepped in. "That's very kind of you to say, but I don't see how that's an appropriate thing to say in this situation."

Awkwardness drifted through the air like a ship lost at sea. Embarrassment engulfed Shawna and Josh's faces. Austin handed the card to Josh without saying a word. Reluctantly, he took it and shoved it in the back pocket of his faded blue jeans.

"Can we forget this ever happened… please?" Shawana tried to put the awkward moment behind them and move forward with a more lighthearted conversation. "I heard that tomorrow is supposed to be one of the warmest days of the summer."

"Um… I think that it might be a good idea if we go out into the hall to talk." Kim didn't want to forget what had just happened, but she didn't want

Austin to hear the conversation that was inevitably going to take place.

Josh and Shawna filed into the hallway followed by Kim and Ben. Kim shut the door to Austin's room so that he wouldn't be able to hear them talking.

"Please explain to me why you did that? Don't get me wrong, it seems like you meant well, but Austin doesn't have a future set in stone" Kim tried to maintain a personable demeanor, but she was dipping into a pool of frustration.

Shawna quickly spoke up, "I don't know what we were thinking. It was inappropriate to say that to Austin especially since he might feel insecure about the surgery… and his life."

"Maybe you thought that by saying that to Austin it would comfort him and make him feel like he does have an amazing life ahead of him. Perhaps you felt like you had over compensate for his illness, but he would really just appreciate a simple prayer." Ben was surprised at the wise words coming out of his mouth since those were usually reserved for Kim.

"Please accept our apologies. We really did mean well, it just came across wrong." Josh held his hand out to Ben.

Ben shook it in an act of brotherly love and forgiveness. "No hard feelings, but I don't know if Austin will want to see you again tonight."

"We should probably get going anyway." Shawna's eyes were silently begging for Kim's forgiveness.

Before they left Kim pulled Shawna in for a hug and whispered in her ear. "I forgive you, and I'll let Austin know you meant well."

"Thank you."

Josh and Shawna left the hospital hand in hand. Kim and Ben rejoined Austin in his room. Austin had been flipping through the devotional that he'd just gotten. His head had started to hurt, so he closed his eyes. When he opened them agian the room looked like it was spinning in circles. He broke out into a violent coughing fit that made his body shake.

"Austin?? Look at me honey, look at me." Kim was kneeling next to Austin's bed, her arm resting on his shoulder.

Austin was gasping for air when his body suddenly went limp. The coughing stopped and his eyes snapped shut. Ben grabbed a nurse who was passing in the hallway.

"Sir, how can I help you?" The nurse was polite and patient towards Ben.

"My son, he's not okay. Could you help him?"

"What happened?" The nurse stepped into the room and started to check Austin's vital signs.

"He was coughing a lot and then he passed out." Ben struggled to find the words to explain what had happened.

"His pulse is a little high, but other than that his vitals seem okay. I think you should call your doctor and let them know what happened. For now it would be best to let him rest."

"Thank you."

The nurse smiled at Ben as she walked away. Kim brushed the back of her hand against Austin's warm forehead. She sat down next to Ben and leaned against him for support.

"He's going to be okay." Ben tried to offer comfort to his wife.

"I know, but it's just hard to see him like this. I'll call Doctor Davis in the morning, maybe he can move the transplant up."

Ben was silent. As the night crept in he and Kim fell asleep in the stiff hospital chairs. Kim woke up before Ben, and after checking to see if Austin was awake she went to the cafeteria to get a cup of coffee. There were only a few people in the seating area and the huge windows revealed a glorious sunrise. Kim stirred creamer into her cup. After taking a long swig of the hot liquid she pulled out her phone and called Doctor Davis. It went to voicemail, so Kim left a message explaining what had happened with Austin.

She walked back to the room, more ready than ever for Austin to be out of the hospital and back home. When she got to his room, Ben was looking at his phone and Austin was sitting up in bed.

"Austin! You're awake!" Relief lit up Kim's face when she saw Austin's eyes.

"Yep." Austin's voice was shaky and he looked weaker than he had since day one of his diagnosis.

Claire came into the room with a glass of water and a tray full of medical equipment. Austin silently groaned because he knew this meant more tests and more needles. He took the water from Claire as if it had become a routine. Kim stepped aside to allow Claire space to perform the tests that continued to make Austin look weaker.

"All done. I hope you feel better soon, and I want you to know that I've never seen someone in your circumstances as joyful as you." Claire offered Austin a sympathetic smile.

"Thanks for saying that. I have Jesus to thank for that." Austin coughed after each word, but he continued to have a willingness to share his faith.

"Get some rest. I'll be back to check on you later. No needles next time, I promise."

"Bye." Austin weakly waved as Claire left to attend to her other patients. "Mom, I'm going to take a nap. It's the only time when everything doesn't hurt."

Austin craved sleep because he could go to a place where every breath didn't feel like a chore. In his dreams he could float on clouds and run like a cheeta, but when he woke up to reality all he could do was sit in bed.

"Okay honey, Doctor Davis will be here soon." Kim kissed Austin on the forehead and watched him gently close his eyes.

An hour later Steve knocked on the doorframe and stepped into the room. He tapped Austin on the shoulder to wake him up. Austin was still groggy, but he sat up and greeted Steve.

"How are you feeling today?" Steve looked as if he had stayed up all night working and a beard had started to form on the bottom half of his face.

"I'm tired." Austin's tone was full of frustration and exhaustion. "How much longer until the surgery?"

"I think I can move it up to Sunday afternoon. The surgeon can come by tomorrow to talk with you and your parents about the procedures."

"Sunday sounds perfect." Austin was ready to get the transplant over with so he could move on with his life.

Being hospitalized was a part of his story that he would never forget, but it didn't need to last forever. Steve left Austin to discuss the surgery with Kim and Ben. Amidst the silence, Austin prayed for God to bring him peace as he struggled to grasp the idea that he would have to undergo a life saving surgery and if it failed it could be the end. Austin waited for an answer of some kind to reassure him that it would all be alright, but nothing came.

Austin closed his eyes and before he knew it he was asleep yet again. Steve had left a while ago, but Kim and Ben stayed in the hallway to talk about what they could do for Austin.

"There's one thing that I know Austin would want more than anything before his surgery, but I don't know how to get it." Ben hadn't given up trying to get ahold of John Anderson, but he was tired of getting the same response.

"Meeting Pastor Anderson would make Austin really happy, but if you can't make it happen don't beat yourself up about it." Kim had tried to tell Ben it was okay to give it a rest before, but he wouldn't take no for an answer.

"If I don't get a response back tonight, I'll go to his office tomorrow morning and he won't have a choice except to come and see my son who is on his deathbed." A spark had gone off inside of Ben. "I want to know that my pastor cares for those who need someone to be there for them in a time of need."

"You can do whatever you want, but don't tell Austin, I don't want him to get excited for nothing."

Ben agreed to make John's pending visit a surprise for Austin, but with his determination, nothing would stop him.

08

John called Bree to come down to the kitchen before he left for the office. She was still wearing her pajamas and the sun was barely peeking through the clouds.

"Are you leaving already?" Bree kissed John before sitting down at the kitchen table.

"My flight for Texas leaves in a few hours and I still have to run to the office to get some papers I forgot to bring home last night. At this rate I'll be surprised if I don't miss the plane."

"You've had close calls before, but you should still get going. Although, I would like it a lot better if you didn't have to go at all." Bree smiled playfully at her husband.

"Me too." John offered his wife a short kiss before pulling away. "I'm leaving now. I love you and I'll text when my flight lands in Texas. Bye!"

Bree leaned against the doorframe that led to the garage as John got in his car. She waved until he was out of sight. The grassy green rolling country hills painted a beautiful scene for John as he sped down the highway to his office.

Ellie was already hard at work when he got there. “Hey John! Don’t you have a plane to catch?”

“Yeah, I have to grab some papers for my speech at the conference. I forgot to stick them in my briefcase yesterday after work.” John unlocked the door to his office and quickly located the papers he’d left behind.

“Hurry! I hope you have a safe flight. I’ve got everything covered here while you're gone.” Ellie’s words offered the reassurance that John always liked to hear.

“I’m off! Make sure not to get into trouble!” John joked with Ellie as he hurried back to his car.

Ellie continued to work for an hour or so when she heard a knock on the door. “Come in!”

A man opened the door and stepped inside the tiny office. “Hello, my name is Ben O’Conors and I would really like to speak with Pastor Anderson.”

“I’m so sorry, you just missed him.”

“You’ve got to be kidding.” Ben muttered under his breath “Where is he?”

"He's probably still at the airport, his flight leaves in a little less than an hour." Ellie paused for a moment, trying to figure out why the man in front of her was so desperate to meet John. "I feel like I know you from somewhere. Why is that?"

"I've emailed you four or five times about getting in touch with Pastor Anderson. My son is dying, and he would really like to meet the man who inspired him to want to be a pastor." Ben choked back the tears that threatened to spill over.

"If you hurry you might be able to catch him before takeoff, I'll write down the gate number so you can find him." Ellie felt the urge to help Ben in any way possible.

"Thank you, I really appreciate this." Ben took the piece of paper that Ellie had scribbled the gate number on to and he ran to his car.

As soon as he got to the airport, Ben ran to the security checkpoint and found the man in charge.

"I don't have a ticket, but I need to get through. My brother is the head of security at this airport, and he'll vouch for me." Ben tried to convince the bulky man standing in front of him to let him by.

"Juan is your brother? I guess you kind of look alike." The man contemplated whether or not to let Ben pass.

"Please, I would never ask unless it was an emergency." Ben pleaded with the man.

"Fine. I'll let you through, but if you step foot on any plane in this airport there will be major consequences, and I'm going to call Juan right now to see if your story checks out. I'm also sending a guard with you to make sure you don't try anything.

Ben let out a huge sigh of relief. "You have no idea how much this means to me."

He pushed past the security line and ran through the gates until he found the one that John was supposed to be at. It looked like they had started to board the plane, so Ben scanned the area for John. After a minute he spotted him sitting with his back to the window that looked out onto the tarmac.

"Pastor Anderson! I have to talk to you." Ben rushed over to John.

"I have a plane to board." John glanced at his watch. "Can you make it quick?"

Ben started to spew out Austin's entire story as quickly as he could. Tears had began to roll down his cheeks, but he didn't care. All that mattered was convincing John to go see Austin.

"His surgery is tomorrow, and there's a chance that… he might not make it. If he could just meet you… it would mean the world to him." Ben pleaded with John as if he were pleading with Death itself.

"I'm supposed to speak at a conference that thousands of people are attending. I can't just not go." John was looking for a reason to say "no" to Ben.

"Please…" Ben blinked back a wave of tears. "You don't know what it's like to not be able to do anything for your son except try to make a wish come true. There will be other conferences, but this is my son's only chance."

John internally fought with himself for the decision he was about to make. “I’ll come meet your son, but let’s go now before I change my mind.”

“Thank you. Thank you so much.” Ben gave John Austin’s room number as they walked out to the parking garage.

“I’ll see you at the hospital in a few minutes.” John stuck his carry-on suitcase in his trunk and waved to Ben.

Austin was reading his Bible when Ben and John got to the room. Ben had asked John to wait outside the room for a minute while he went in to talk to Austin.

“Austin, I brought you a visitor.” Ben tried to hide the smile that threatened to take over his face.

“I’m not really in the mood to see anyone.” Austin shut his book and sunk lower into the bed that had been his best friend for the past few weeks.

“You’ll like this visitor.” Ben motioned for John to come in.

The second that John stepped into the room Austin's jaw dropped. "Pastor Anderson?"

Ben left the room to give Austin and John some space.

Austin's throat suddenly felt very dry and he struggled to find the words to say. "I can't believe that you're here. I love watching you preach…"

"Your dad told me all about how you like to sit in the front row every Sunday and how you want to be a pastor when you get a little older. Is that right?" John started to feel a joy that he hadn't felt in a very long time.

"Yeah, you've inspired me to pursue my dreams of being a pastor. When I get out of this hospital, I'm going to do everything I can to start reaching that goal."

"I don't think I've ever met someone your age with that much commitment to anything, much less becoming a pastor. That shows real maturity." John started to grasp just how much every word he said would impact Austin.

"Thank you." Austin's face beamed with so much color and joy that it would be hard to tell he was sick at all.

Over the next hour, John spent time asking Austin questions and getting to know him better. Before he left, John offered to pray for Austin, and Austin immediately accepted.

John rested his hand on Austin's shoulder and started to pray. "Heavenly Father, I don't think I've ever met someone as joyful as Austin is right now. Thank you for this boy's heart for you and his passion to share Jesus with others. I pray that you would heal Austin completely and that you would guide the hands of the surgeons tomorrow as they give Austin new lungs. Thank you for the opportunity to meet this young man, Amen."

"Thanks for praying for me." Austin couldn't believe that John Anderson had just spent an hour talking with him.

"No problem kiddo. Hopefully I'll see you in church soon." John's heart felt more full than it had in months. It had taken meeting someone like Austin to bring him back to life.

"Bye Pastor Anderson." Austin was sad to see John go, but he was more glad that he'd come in the first place.

After John left, Kim and Ben joined Austin. There was still a smile on Austin's face, but he looked like he'd just come inside after being stuck in a blizzard all day.

"Are you feeling alright? You look kind of pale." Kim felt Austin's forehead to see if it was warm. "You're burning up!"

She motioned for Ben to go find Claire. Ben dashed out of the room and Kim forced Austin to take a sip of water. When Ben came back with Claire his cheeks were flushed from running around the hospital in a frenzy. Claire took Autin's temperature and tried to hide the results from Kim. The thermometer had indicated that Austin had a fever of 105.7, and Claire knew that not telling Kim would be better for Austin.

"He has a fever. I'll make sure he's getting enough fluids, but I don't think there's anything else I can do." Claire looked at the monitor connected to Austin's IV. "Ben, could I see you in the hallway for a second."

"Uh… sure. Do you need Kim too?"

"It would be better if she stayed with Austin." Claire stepped into the hall.

Ben stood across from Claire, trying to read her. "Something's wrong. What is it? Is that why you told Kim to stay with Austin because you knew she would freak out if she knew?"

"Yes. I've done everything I can, but I don't know if Austin's going to make it through the night. He has a very high fever and he's not breathing enough. Even if he made it to the surgery tomorrow, he's so sick with other things that it might be worse to put him through that." Claire tried to be as gentle and sympathetic as possible while delivering the news.

"Should we… call Doctor Davis?" Ben felt like he was in shock…this was the moment he'd been praying would never come, but now it had and he wasn't prepared to say goodbye to his son.

"I'll call him, you go spend time with Austin and let Kim know."

Ben silently returned to Austin's room and the look on his face told Kim everything she needed to know. Ben nodded before Kim even had a chance to ask.

"Austin…Can you look at me?" Kim couldn't see through the tears that had clouded her vision. Her voice was shaky and she had to sit down to keep from falling over.

"I'm dying, aren't I? I was so close to the surgery… so close." The effort it took Austin to speak made him feel completely exhausted.

"Know that I love you more than anything in this world. You make me smile when I feel like crying and you are the best son a mother could ever ask for." Kim tried to stay strong for Austin, but she was struggling to bear the pain of losing her only son.

Ben knelt beside Austin and let his stone hard face soften into a compassionate smile. “My son, I love you so much. I never was good at showing you how very much I cared about you, but I do. I’ve loved every second I’ve spent with you and you will always be my son.”

“Why do I have to go? I’m not ready… I never got to be a pastor. I want to stay here.” Austin had tears streaming down his colorless face.

“God holds the whole world in His hands, and that includes you. If this is a part of his plan, there’s a reason.” Ben tried to offer comfort to Austin during his dying moments.

“I love you guys. Can we please pray together?” Austin’s eyes were wide and glazed over with tears.

“Of course. Go ahead.” Kim rested her hand on top of Austin’s.

He whispered into the silence. “God… please take care of Mom and Dad. If you want me to come home to you then so be it, but it’s not fair to them, so please take care of them.”

Austin didn't expect a response, but as he cried out to God he felt an overwhelming sense of peace like nothing he'd ever felt in his life. He weakly tried to say something to his parents, but all that came out was a hoarse, uneven breath, the words at the tip of his tongue fading and being lost in the endless chasm that is death. He closed his eyes and squeezed his mom's hand for the last time. The machines that had been keeping him alive let out a harrowing beep.

Kim fell to her knees and cried harder than she had in a long time. Ben joined her on the ground with a heavy heart. Claire heard the monitors go off and she walked in to find Kim and Ben weeping together on the ground. She maneuvered around them to pull a sheet over Austin's motionless body. Claire unplugged all of the machines that were going off and left the room until all that could be heard was the sound of Kim's grievous crying.

Within the week a funeral was held and Kim was able to smile again because she knew that Austin was dancing with Jesus. Ben had been going through Austin's room and he found the boxes of letters that Austin had written to John over the past two or so years.

He'd been tempted to read them but Kim convinced him not to and to give them to John instead. It had been a little over two weeks since Austin's death, and it was the first time Kim and Ben had been back to church since the hospitalization. After the service Ben was able to locate John. Kim had brought the boxes of letters with them to give to John.

"Hey… I heard about Austin, and I'm so, so, sorry. I honestly have to thank him because I've been going through a rough patch lately and meeting Austin was God's way of saying a lot of things to me that I needed to hear." John had been praying constantly after he'd visited Austin and everyone had noticed a change.

"We have something to give you." Kim held out the old shoebox. "It's something that we found in Austin's room. We think that he wrote you a letter every Saturday and never had the opportunity to give them to you so he kept them in a shoebox under his bed."

John took the box from Kim, but words escaped him. He gently removed the lid to reveal stacks of envelopes with his name written on the front. John grabbed one off the top and opened it. There was a long message thanking John, asking questions, and simply talking about what was going on in Austin's life.

"This is touching… I don't know what to say." John dabbed the corners of his eyes with the back of his sleeve. "No one has ever taken this much time to do something so meaningful for me. I wish Austin was here so I could thank him."

"I'm glad you like it. I'm sure Austin would have been thrilled to know that the letters got to you." Ben was glad that he'd been able to deliver the letters to John because they had obviously made an impact.

"If you two will excuse me, I have some reading to do." John grabbed the box and took it with him to his office.

He sat down in his leather swivel chair with his head bowed in silence. The letters were sitting untouched on his desk. John was deep in thought, but was interrupted when Ellie knocked on the door.

"John, it's getting late. I'm going to go home now."

"Huh?" John looked up and checked the time on his phone. "It is late. Go home, thanks for letting me know."

Ellie nodded and headed off to her car. John packed up his stuff and carefully tucked the box of letters under his arm. Bree was sitting at the kitchen table waiting for him when he got home.

"How was church today?" Bree sensed that something was bothering John.

"That boy who I met a few weeks ago… His parents gave me something they found in his room." John sat down across from Bree.

"What is it?"

"A box full of letters that he wrote to me every Saturday night for at least two years." John set the box down in between him and Bree. “Every Saturday…”

John still couldn’t get over the fact that someone looked up to him that much. Bree fingered through the letters and pulled one of them from the middle of the stack. She took it out of the envelope and scanned through it.

“This is long.” She set it back in the box.

“I know, they’re all long. I wish I would’ve met him sooner. Then again, maybe it was better I met him when I did…”

A week later, John walked out onto the sleek, black stage as he’d done for countless Sunday’s. Before the lights went up he glanced into the audience to see if he could spot Kim and Ben. They were sitting in the front row, right where Austin would always sit.

“Good morning, I’d like to start this week's sermon out with full transparency. I’ve been struggling lately, but I thought it was best to shove my problems in a box and then lock it up so no one could see. However, the past few weeks have taught me that the best way to deal with my problems is to share them."

John opened his Bible that was sitting on a tall table next to him. "I had the pleasure of meeting a boy who was very sick. In fact, I learned that he'd passed away shortly after I met him. Needless to say, it was one of the most important encounters I've had. This boy helped me to realize that I was lost. God has placed me in a position to shepherd the congregation of this church, to act as a leader for those who need guidance. But, I myself needed some shepherding."

John watched the crowd as he tried to open up to thousands of people who knew him better than he knew any of them. "I was a lost shepherd, but God showed me, through a boy who was face to face with death, that I don't have to be lost. God reached down and pulled me out of my sin and into the light. He allowed me to see that I was messing up, but he also helped to show me that there's a way to be found. I'm no longer a lost shepherd, I'm his, and it's the most beautiful thing in the world..."

The End.

Made in the USA
Monee, IL
24 May 2022

96983249R00085